JACOB WONDERBAR
and the interstellar time warp

nathan bransford

illustrated by C.S. Jennings

Dial Books for Young Readers
an imprint of Penguin Group (USA) Inc.

DIAL BOOKS FOR YOUNG READERS
A division of Penguin Young Readers Group
Published by The Penguin Group
Penguin Group (USA) Inc., 375 Hudson Street, New York, NY 10014, U.S.A.
Penguin Group (Canada), 90 Eglinton Avenue East, Suite 700, Toronto, Ontario, Canada M4P 2Y3 (a
division of Pearson Penguin Canada Inc.)
Penguin Books Ltd, 80 Strand, London WC2R 0RL, England
Penguin Ireland, 25 St. Stephen's Green, Dublin 2, Ireland
(a division of Penguin Books Ltd)
Penguin Group (Australia), 707 Collins Street, Melbourne, Victoria 3008,
Australia (a division of Pearson Australia Group Pty Ltd)
Penguin Books India Pvt Ltd, 11 Community Centre,
Panchsheel Park, New Delhi—110 017, India
Penguin Group (NZ), 67 Apollo Drive, Rosedale, Auckland 0632,
New Zealand (a division of Pearson New Zealand Ltd)
Penguin Books (South Africa), Rosebank Office Park, 181 Jan Smuts Avenue,
Parktown North 2193, South Africa
Penguin China, B7 Jiaming Center, 27 East Third Ring Road North,
Chaoyang District, Beijing 100020,
Penguin Books Ltd, Registered Offices: 80 Strand,
London WC2R 0RL, England

Designed by Jasmin Rubero
Text set in Breughel Com
Printed in the U.S.A.

1 3 5 7 9 10 8 6 4 2

Library of Congress Cataloging-in-Publication Data
Bransford, Nathan.
Jacob Wonderbar and the interstellar time warp /
Nathan Bransford ; illustrated by C. S. Jennings.
p. cm.
Summary: In the two weeks twelve-year-old Jacob Wonderbar was away, fifty years have passed on Earth
and now he, Sarah Daisy, and Dexter, with help from
Mick Cracken, try to set things right by seeking Jacob's father, who is lost in time.
ISBN 978-0-8037-3703-7 (hardback)
[1. Space and time—Fiction. 2. Interplanetary voyages—Fiction.
3. Adventure and adventurers—Fiction. 4. Fathers and sons—Fiction.
5. Science fiction.] I. Jennings, C. S., ill. II. Title.
PZ7.B73755Jai 2013   [Fic]—dc23   2012020967

JACOB WONDERBAR

Chapter 1

Jacob Wonderbar had only been gone for two weeks, long enough to run for president of the universe, lose the election, save the Planet Earth, and fly back home aboard the spaceship Praiseworthy. But instead of returning to his normal life of planning pranks and shooting hoops after school and pretending he enjoyed his mother's adventures in cooking, he was face-to-face with a ninety-year-old version of his mom.

Only Jacob was still twelve years old.

Jacob's mother squeezed his shoulder.

"You have to find your father," she said. "You've been gone for fifty years."

It couldn't be happening. It had only been two weeks. And yet somehow half a century had passed on Earth.

His mom took another step toward him. She pressed her wrinkled lips together in thought. He backed away and felt the doorknob jab his spine. He couldn't get any farther away unless he ran out the door.

"I'm so happy to see you!" She smiled. "I don't think I've had a happier day in all my life."

Jacob searched his brain for words. They hadn't returned to Earth in a time machine, they had flown home on Praiseworthy. He couldn't explain it. "But . . . what happened? Why are you old?"

His mom smiled sweetly. "I aged the normal way, one day at a time." Her eyes crinkled. "I missed you so much."

Jacob's heart swelled as he imagined his mom staring out the window and hoping every single day that he would come home. There would have been a frantic search in the beginning followed by disappointment, and then days that became weeks that became months that became years that became decades, one long day at a time. All those years wondering what happened to him, all those long afternoons holding out hope that maybe, somehow he was just lost somewhere and would come home. Fifty years of waiting. He rushed forward and hugged his mom. He didn't care how scary she looked.

"Where's Dad? How am I going to find him?"

Jacob's mom rested her hand on his shoulder to calm him down. "I don't know, Jacob. All I know is that your father will know what happened."

"But . . ."

Jacob's mother shook her head. "I don't have the answers, Jacob. I'm not sure what happened. I hate to send you back out, but you have to set things right."

Jacob steeled his resolve. He could do this.

His mom stared at him with intense eyes. "I'm depending on you, Jacob. This isn't the life we're supposed to be living. I know that. I should have been able to watch you grow up and see all of the great things in your future. My world has been darker without you. The whole world has been darker."

"But . . ."

"Go, Jacob. Go. I'll see you in the past."

Jacob turned to the door.

"Oh," his mom said. "And I don't think the younger me will be much help."

He wasn't sure what she meant, but he knew he had to go. He hugged his mom again and nodded.

"I'll fix it."

Chapter 2

Jacob ran out the door and down the street. The sidewalks were cracked and sprouted spindly yellow weeds. The streetlamps were broken and the street was unnaturally dark.

He nearly collided with Sarah Daisy.

"Jake!" she shouted.

"Sarah! What's happening?"

"There are strangers living in my house! I think they kidnapped my parents!" Sarah looked around in fear and then hugged Jacob. "Where are we?" she asked into his shoulder. "What happened?!"

"Sarah, my mom is old." Jacob broke the hug. "Like, *old*. I think fifty years have gone by. She said I have to find my dad."

"Fifty years?! How is that possible?"

"I don't know."

It had been terrifying to arrive at home and find his mother significantly older, but Jacob was thankful that she still lived in the same house and he was able to speak with her. They had *something* to go on, even if it was just the smallest scrap of an idea. At least Jacob knew he had to find his dad.

On the other hand, Jacob had spent a lifetime searching for his dad and hadn't ever come close to finding him. Not even running for president of the universe had brought his dad out into the open.

"Guys?" they heard a tentative voice say from a short distance away.

"Yeah, it's us, Dexter," Sarah said.

Dexter slunk up to them and stared at them for a moment in the darkness. "Something is amiss," he said.

Sarah couldn't help but laugh. "You think?"

"My house looks like it has ghosts living in it! My parents changed the locks and no one's home."

"We're in the future," Sarah said.

Jacob took a deep breath. He had been looking forward to returning to being a kid again, to hanging out with Sarah and Dexter and having fun. He wasn't sure he was ready for another adventure.

But adventure had found him. Jacob knew there

was only one way to find out how fifty Earth years could have gone by in two weeks. They had to go back to space.

"Come on," Jacob said. "Let's go find Praiseworthy."

Sarah and Dexter looked at each other and grimaced. They walked back toward the forest down the street, and Jacob felt a stirring of excitement that he would soon be flying between the stars once again. Still, he stopped himself from smiling in front of Sarah and Dexter because they were so worried.

"Jumping jellybeans!" the spaceship Praiseworthy exclaimed when they stepped on board. "Children, I didn't expect you back so soon, this is quite a pleasure!"

Jacob could feel Sarah's and Dexter's expectant gazes and their hope that he'd have a plan to set things right. He didn't really know what to do or where he could find his dad or who had sent them fifty years into the future. But when solving a mystery, he figured it made sense to start with the prime suspect.

And Mick Cracken was always Suspect Number One.

"Praiseworthy," Jacob said. "Please take us to Planet Royale."

Chapter 3

Ten Earth hours later, Praiseworthy touched
down outside the presidential palace on Planet
Royale. At first glance the palace didn't look very
much changed in the intervening fifty years, and for a
moment Jacob wondered whether time had somehow
passed only on Earth.

But as they walked through the garden, Jacob noticed
some changes. There were several statues of a young
man in outlandish poses. In one, he was bowing with an
oversized hat, and in another he was diving to one side
and shooting two blasters at once. Jacob had a sneaking
suspicion they were depicting an older Mick Cracken.

They paused for a moment at the palace doors, and
then Sarah knocked. A moment later a regal woman
with fine dark hair opened the door, and when they

asked for Mick Cracken, she led the children down the hall with a kind smile.

Jacob kept glancing out of the corner of his eyes, waiting for one of Mick Cracken's tricks. All he saw instead were more and more paintings of a twenty-something man with an uncanny resemblance to Mick.

"Ha-ha!" they heard a man laugh. "Ha!"

Though the voice was deeper, Jacob knew immediately who it belonged to.

Mick Cracken stepped around the corner. Only, instead of the twelve-year-old version they had last seen, he was older, taller, nearly bald, extremely rotund, and looked wildly pleased with himself.

"I've been waiting for this moment for fifty years. Fifty years! Do you know how long that is? Hang on." He closed his eyes and took a deep breath, barely able to contain his excitement. "I need to enjoy this moment. Ah. There. It really is great to be me."

Sarah Daisy cleared her throat and Mick opened his eyes. "Get to the point," she said.

Mick sniffed and looked down his nose at her. "Your attitude hasn't changed a bit."

"It's been one day!" Sarah said.

"Cracken," Jacob said. "Why don't you skip to the part where you tell us what you did?"

Mick walked over and stared down at Jacob, enjoying that he was taller than him. "Not until I've finished gloating."

"Aren't you a little old for that?" Sarah asked, crossing her arms.

Mick grunted. "You sound like my wife."

Sarah nearly fainted at the idea that Mick was married.

"Can I get you children anything?" the lady said. "You've come a long way, you must be so exhausted."

"Can we get rid of him?" Sarah said, jerking her thumb at Mick.

The lady laughed and whispered to Sarah, "He *is* pretty annoying, isn't he?"

"You're one to talk!" Mick shouted.

"Could I pick out some new clothes for you, perhaps?" the lady asked. "You have obviously been through quite an ordeal if you were forced to wear those sad rags."

Sarah looked down at her jeans and sweatshirt. "Oh, no."

"What?" Dexter said.

"Don't you see who this is?" Sarah asked through her teeth.

Jacob looked at the lady again and realized it was

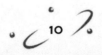

Catalina Crackenarium, Mick's sister and former princess. Only she was a grown-up.

"Cat?" Jacob said, feeling strange calling an older lady by such a familiar name. He wondered if he should be calling her "Mrs. Cat."

"Of course it's me, silly!" Catalina said. She clapped happily. "This is so fun! Though I must say I'm surprised that you're still hanging around this one." She jerked her thumb at Sarah, who turned bright red.

Jacob and Sarah stared at each other for a moment, not knowing what to say. It was too strange for words. But Jacob finally found his voice.

"Cracken, where's my dad? You know where he is, don't you?"

Mick's smile vanished, and for a fleeting moment something approaching sympathy crossed his face. He glanced over at Catalina, who looked similarly worried. Mick seemed like an adult all of a sudden, someone who was responsible enough to be concerned for a person's well-being.

"Well . . . Wondersomething . . ." Mick said.

"Wonderbar," Jacob said.

"Your dad is lost in time. And you're the only one who can find him."

Chapter 4

Mick moved a graffiti painting from the wall, unlocked and opened a safe, pulled out a wooden chest, unlocked it, pulled out a smaller metal chest, unlocked that, and then finally pulled out a large key. He held it out in front of the children. It looked like an old skeleton key made of rough iron, though it was large and looked heavy.

"This is the most valuable item in the entire universe."

"It looks like a big key," Dexter said.

"Well, it's important!" Mick said. "There are people who would blow up galaxies for this." He tapped Jacob and Dexter on the nose and tried to do the same to Sarah, but she batted away his hand. "Don't. Lose. This. Key."

"Okay . . ." Jacob said. "It's a key. So what?"

Mick ignored Jacob's question. "When Father Albert created the Astral colonies, he decided to send the small group of original Astrals back in time ten thousand years so they'd multiply and develop new technologies and be ready in case Earth ever wanted to bring war to space. By the time Earthers developed their own pitiful excuses for spaceships and rockets, Astrals were already way more advanced and living all around the galaxy. He gave us a history."

"Okay, great. You have time travel," Sarah said. "So why did you send us fifty years into the future?"

Mick stepped over and looked at a painting of a spaceship. "In the early days of the Astral colonies, time travel was a way of life. If Astrals overcooked their dinner, they'd go back in time to fix it. If they needed to play a good prank on their neighbor, they'd go back in time and mess with their plumbing. But all that back and forth throughout time got really, really confusing. People would forget what day they were supposed to be living in, then they would run into their past and future selves, get into arguments with them . . . it got super-awkward. So the decision was made: No more time travel. Everyone would have to go back to eating burned toast and flying around the galaxy in spaceships like normal people."

"Only you seem to have a special time travel key," Dexter said.

"Yes," Mick said, waving the key and looking very pleased. "Throughout Astral history, there were only two people who were allowed to time travel. One was the king, my father, who kept a few of the old time travel relics from the early days. I believe you experienced one of those on your first space trip. The other was the Timekeeper, the person in charge of making sure there were no unauthorized trips through time. The Timekeeper has been an extremely important person throughout Astral history. He or she is the person responsible for tracking, stopping, and fixing illegal time travel. And for obvious reasons their identity was always completely top-secret, known only to the king. And now the president. Me."

"How are you still president after fifty years?" Sarah asked.

Mick puffed out his huge belly. "I'm very good at my job. I've only lost six elections."

"Can we get this Timekeeper person to find my dad?" Jacob asked.

Mick blinked. "Um. Your dad *was* the Timekeeper. And now he's missing."

Jacob's jaw dropped.

"My dad?"

Mick nodded. "Yes."

"*My* dad? As in . . . my dad?"

Mick looked around the room. "Do you have hearing problems? Yes, Wonderbark, your dad."

"Wonderbar," Jacob said absently.

Jacob couldn't picture his dad as an important person, let alone one of the most important people in the entire universe. His dad couldn't manage something as simple as a trip to the supermarket without turning it into a huge catastrophe, and he couldn't imagine how the Astrals could have entrusted him with something as crucial as making sure time unfolded like it was supposed to. Jacob had the sudden sense that there was more to his dad than he ever knew.

Mick waved the key. "Here's how it works. You'll need to specify a place *and* time. Say it out loud to the key, then say 'Warp' when you're ready to warp. If you're going in a group, everyone needs to be touching the key or touching another person who is touching the key. Now listen closely, because this is important. When you change the past, it can have huge, massive changes on the future. All those little things that you went back and did can have very big repercussions. You'll never know what they're going to be. So be very, very careful. Understood?"

"Got it." Dexter nodded.

"Are you sure?"

"Yes," Dexter said.

"Are you all completely one hundred and ten percent sure?"

No one answered. Instead Jacob lunged at Mick and grabbed on to the key. He sensed that Mick was setting them up for a trap, and Jacob wanted to be the one to decide where they were going in time. Mick tried to shrug him off, but Jacob held on tightly. He grunted with the effort.

"Guys!" Jacob shouted. "Grab on!"

Sarah and Dexter leaped in and started pulling on the key as well.

"My house, May second, 2012, four p.m.!" Jacob shouted. "Warp!"

Jacob felt the air rush out of his lungs. He closed his eyes tightly as every color came rushing into his brain at once. He felt his stomach drop, then he opened his eyes and saw his front door with the familiar faded wreath.

"Whoa," Dexter said.

They all looked around for a moment before realizing they were still holding on to the key. They all started pulling again, each trying to pry it free. Jacob kicked Mick in the shins over and over and Dexter bit his wrist.

"Ow!" Mick shouted. Finally he let go and Jacob stashed the key in his jeans.

Mick limped around trying to regain feeling in his legs. He stopped and sniffed the air. "Where are we?"

"Earth, dummy," Sarah said.

Mick's face screwed up as if he had just tasted something rather disgusting. "I don't like the way this place smells."

"Move along down the road," Jacob said.

Mick rubbed his large belly, his eyes wide with worry. "You're just going to leave me here? On *Earth*?"

"That's right," Jacob said.

"But I'm on your side!" Mick said.

Jacob laughed.

Mick sighed and looked at the sky. "Can't people change?"

"I don't think so," Sarah said.

Mick stared at them for a moment and then charged at Jacob. Dexter deftly stuck out his leg and tripped him and Mick went sprawling onto the grass like a fallen elephant. He stood up, brushed himself off, and scratched his chin. Then he smiled. "This is all going according to my plan. I want you to have the key."

"Sure you do," Sarah said.

Mick narrowed his eyes, bowed, and walked away.

"Good riddance," Sarah muttered.

"See you in the past!" Mick shouted over his shoulder. "I'm counting on you."

Chapter 5

So what do we do with this?" Jacob asked. "Where should we start looking for my dad?"

Sarah looked at her feet and then glanced down the street. She kicked her toe on the ground and twirled it around. "Jake, I want to help find your dad. That is absolutely our number one priority. Like, completely number one. Right, Dexter?"

Dexter nodded. "Affirmative."

Sarah looked at the ground. "But I really miss my family. I haven't seen them in weeks."

"But it's technically the same day we left! They don't even know you've been gone."

"You know what I mean," Sarah mumbled.

"But . . ." Jacob started. He turned away from them a moment and stared at the door to his house. He thought about his grandfather's pipe, the heirloom he had found in outer space on his first voyage. And he remembered how he felt when the king of the universe had told him he was half Astral. He had been consumed with the mystery of his missing dad for so long. He was closer than ever to finding out what happened and now he had the time machine to go searching.

But he didn't even know where to begin to look. He needed to find some clues. It occurred to him that he could start searching at home.

"Wonderbar," Dexter said gently, pointing at the time machine. "We have all the time in the world."

Jacob nodded. "Okay. You're right. Let's go spend some time with our families and meet in the forest at sunset. And then we can go looking for my dad."

Sarah punched Jacob softly on the shoulder and Dexter patted him on the back.

"We'll find him," Dexter said.

They jogged together down the street in the direction of their houses.

Jacob took a deep breath and walked into his house, bracing himself in case it wasn't really his mom or she was even older. But there she was, in the kitchen, a normal age, and she smiled at him when he came in. His heart flooded with relief.

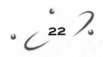

"Perfect timing," she said.

Jacob sat down at the kitchen counter and poked at his mom's latest culinary concoction, a green-and-yellow mess of a dish that Jacob couldn't even identify. He smiled despite himself and knew he'd have to plan a secret meal because there was no way he was going to eat this. He thought about his unfinished business. He wondered how much his mom knew, whether she had been in on the fact that his dad was the Timekeeper or if she knew he had been lost in time.

"Mom, what happened with Dad?" Jacob said.

Jacob's mom froze in place for a second before regaining her bearings. She sat down to face Jacob.

"I'm surprised, darling," she said, "Because normally you don't want to—"

"Where did he go?" Jacob asked. "What happened?"

Jacob's mom looked away for a moment before pressing her hands together and resting them on her chin.

"Honey, it's hard to explain," she said.

"Try," Jacob said. "I need to find him."

Jacob thought back to all the times he had wondered where his dad went, the time he and Sarah found his dad on the Internet and it said he lived in Milwaukee, the postcard his dad sent him, all those missed basketball games and all the times he had to correct people when they mentioned his parents, plural, and he had to say he only had one parent. He always noticed the way they looked away in embarrassment afterward and somehow it made it even worse that they felt sorry for him.

"I don't know how to explain it," Jacob's mom said. "Sometimes you think you know someone, and it turns out you don't."

"What does that mean?" Jacob asked. He wondered if she knew he was from outer space when they were married and if she had been in on it all along, but he couldn't bring himself to speak the words. There was something that still felt so unreal about his dad growing up in space, and he couldn't quite admit to his mom that he knew part of the truth. He wanted to see if she would be honest with him.

Jacob's mom cleared her throat and tapped a finger on the table.

"Mom, tell me the truth. Please. I need to know what happened."

"I don't know what to say, Jacob," his mom said. She sounded sympathetic, but there was edge to her voice that let Jacob know he was on shaky ground. "The past is just the past."

Jacob could tell from her tone that the conversation was over. He would have to find his dad on his own.

Chapter 6

The sun was setting over his street when Jacob jogged toward the forest, his heart pounding with excitement. This time he wouldn't be hopping on a spaceship and blasting off into space. Instead he would be blasting himself back in time.

Jacob imagined the immense power that was resting in his pocket. He could go look at cavemen. He could go see how the future turned out. He could go meet Abraham Lincoln or someone from two hundred years in the future.

He gulped. He could see who was going to win the NBA championship.

"Hey!" Sarah shouted when she saw him. "You ready?"

He found Sarah and Dexter sitting in the clearing in the forest where they used to hang out when they were younger, the same place where they discovered the spaceship Lucy and started their space adventures. Jacob picked up a stick and sat down on a log. The light was dimming in the forest and just a few lazy beams of orange light found their way to the scrubby dirt on the forest floor.

"Well?" Sarah asked. "Where should we go?"

Jacob racked his brain trying to think of where they could warp. He didn't have the faintest clue where to find his father. Neither his mom in the present nor his mom fifty years in the future had been of any help. His dad could be anywhere and any*when* in time. All Jacob knew was that his dad was the Timekeeper, whatever that meant.

"I really don't know," Jacob said.

"Where were your dad's last known whereabouts?" Dexter asked.

Jacob tapped his stick on the ground. "The last time I saw my dad, my parents got in a big fight and he left. I haven't seen him since."

Sarah and Dexter sat very still. A dove cooed somewhere in the trees above and a faint breeze stirred the branches above them.

"We could go see dinosaurs," Sarah finally said. "Dexter, you love dinosaurs more than anyone."

"I like dinosaurs," Dexter said. "But I don't want to get eaten by a T. rex."

"That's the Cretaceous Period," Sarah said. "I would want to go to the Jurassic Period anyway. I want to see an apatosaurus."

Dexter was silent for a moment. "I don't want to be stepped on by an apatosaurus. And there were plenty of scary meat eaters in the Jurassic Period too. Like the allosaurus."

Sarah frowned. "But it would be so cool!"

"Too scary," Dexter said. "What about the future instead? We could see the new inventions and crazy skyscrapers and things."

"I know!" Sarah said. "Let's go back to medieval times and see knights jousting."

"Let's go watch the Egyptians build the pyramids," Dexter said.

"I want to see Michelangelo painting the Sistine Chapel!" Sarah shouted.

"Jacques Cousteau's submarine!"

"Shakespeare!"

"Marco Polo!"

"The Incas!"

"George Washington!"

"Josephine Baker!"

"Guys, come on," Jacob said with a stern tone. "This is a serious choice."

Sarah and Dexter looked a little sheepish, remembering that they had started the discussion by wondering how to find Jacob's dad before they had gotten carried away.

Then Jacob broke out into a wide grin. "Definitely dinosaurs."

Sarah pumped her fists in the air. She jabbed a finger at Dexter.

"Outvoted!" she shouted.

Chapter 1

The children stood around the key. Dexter, their resident dinosaur expert, was responsible for choosing the location.

"Okay," Dexter said. "An apatosaurus fossil was discovered in Wyoming, so I think we should go there." He scratched his chin. "I think. I mean, as long as you guys still think this is a good idea."

"Listen," Jacob said quietly and seriously. "Dexter's right. This could be really dangerous. Stay close together. We're warping back at the first sign of trouble. Agreed?"

Sarah swallowed and nodded. Dexter looked pale but somewhat excited.

They all grabbed the key. Dexter cleared his throat and said, "Key, take us to Casper, Wyoming, 150 million years ago, high noon. Please." He took a deep breath. "Warp!"

The air rushed out of Jacob's lungs, and when he opened his eyes he was staring at a small clearing in front of a lush, gigantic forest. The trees looked a little unusual, like overgrown pine trees, and they soared high into the sky. He took a deep breath of warm, humid air. The ground was covered in leafy greens and ferns. He thought he spotted something flying in the distance, but he couldn't see it clearly through the trees.

He quickly looked around and determined that they weren't in imminent danger, though he couldn't be certain an allosaurus wasn't lurking nearby, ready to eat them for breakfast.

"Do you see anything?" Jacob whispered.

Sarah and Dexter shook their heads.

It occurred to Jacob that finding a dinosaur might be harder than they thought. After all, you don't just walk into a forest and find a bear on your first try.

Jacob stepped through the forest, feeling the soft brush of ferns against his legs. A sharp yellow plant scraped across his arms. He looked around, waiting for a stegosaurus or an allosaurus to come charging out of the forest.

Suddenly a lizard jumped in front of Jacob. It was

about three feet tall, stood on two legs, had scaly dark green skin, and it moved its head around extremely quickly. It darted out and bit an orange flower, spit it out, then grabbed a fern instead and chewed that quickly. One of its eyes stayed locked on the children.

It didn't have sharp teeth. It didn't have cool armored plates on its head. It was just a mildly tall lizard. Jacob was confident they had found the least exciting dinosaur in the Jurassic era. He had seen cooler reptiles at the zoo.

"Othnielia!" Dexter shouted.

"What?" Jacob asked.

Dexter shrugged. "It's an othnielia. It's a plant eater and it runs fast. And . . . That's all I know."

The othnielia pecked at Jacob's knee, recoiled a bit as if it was completely dissatisfied with the taste, and then grabbed another fern. It eyed Jacob suspiciously.

"That's it?" Sarah asked quietly. "This is what we traveled back in time for?"

Jacob heard a rustle in the brush.

"Shh!" he whispered.

The children stood very still. Jacob crouched down behind a bush, and through the branches he saw some tall ferns waving. Something large was approaching. He signaled to Sarah and Dexter to be ready to grab on to the time machine and warp back to the

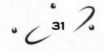

present. Jacob braced himself to see an allosaurus or a velociraptor or a stegosaurus. A part of him hoped they would see the scariest dinosaur imaginable.

The rustling in the ferns moved closer and closer until it was nearly in front of them.

Jacob clutched the key.

Sarah's kid sister, Chloe, aka "The Brat," walked into the clearing and stood in front of them with a big smile.

"Surprise!" Chloe said.

For a moment, Jacob, Dexter, and Sarah were too stunned to speak.

"You?" Sarah finally said.

Chloe looked like a smaller version of Sarah Daisy,

only she had dark hair and was even more animated and energetic than her older sister. She was one and a half years younger than Sarah, and she always tried to sit between Jacob and Sarah during the Daisy family movie night precisely because she knew how much it annoyed Sarah. She possessed a phenomenal talent for convincing her parents that she needed to tag along whenever Sarah and Jacob went out in public, and though Jacob did not have any siblings, he was immensely relieved that he didn't have any like The Brat.

Chloe winked at Dexter and smiled. "Hey, Dexy."

Dexter opened his mouth to speak but seemed incapable of producing any words.

"What are you doing here?!" Sarah shouted.

Chloe's face turned serious.

"I come from the future," she said ominously. Then she tipped back her head and cackled.

Chapter 8

J acob is going to send *you* back in time?" Sarah
asked. "To be here with us. In the Jurassic era.
Why in the world would he do that?"

"Why should I tell you?"

"That's it," Sarah said. "We're taking her back
home."

Dexter looked wistfully around the forest. "But
now that we're here . . ."

"No dinosaurs," Sarah said. She jabbed her thumb at
her sister. "Getting rid of this one is more important."

Chloe held out her hand for Dexter and grinned.
"Here, Dexy," she said. "I found this for you."

She dropped a large claw into Dexter's hand. It
was dark and smooth and looked like it belonged to a

fearsome creature. He turned it over in his hands and tapped his finger on the sharp end.

Chloe leaned in close to Dexter. "I think it's from one of the really scary ones."

Dexter looked at Chloe and was unable to pronounce any words of thanks. He swallowed and took a few deep breaths before finally whispering, "This."

"Oh good lord," Sarah said.

"I don't believe you," Jacob said.

Everyone turned to face Jacob, but his attention was focused squarely on Chloe. She smiled as if she was expecting Jacob's accusations, and she straightened up and furrowed her brow in an overly dramatic fashion.

"Why, Jacob Wonderbar," Chloe said. "What*ever* do you mean?"

"Tell us why you're really here," Jacob said.

"Because," Chloe whined. "Future you said to tell you guys to bring me along with you. Everything depends on it or something."

Jacob glared at her and tried to puzzle out what was happening. His future self wouldn't have sent her back in the past if there wasn't a good reason for it. Surely there was some reason why she had managed to travel several hundred million years in the past just to tag along with them yet again. And she didn't seem to have a time machine, so she couldn't have gone back in time by herself. Someone had left her in the past knowing full well she would run into them.

"Who sent you?" Jacob asked.

"You did!" Chloe said.

"But—"

They heard a deafening hiss behind them in the forest. Jacob froze. Whatever made that noise did not sound friendly.

He slowly looked over his shoulder and saw a massive dinosaur peering down at them. It was as tall as a house and was only twenty yards away. It had a giant head, tiny clawed arms, and stood on gigantic hind legs. It hissed again, revealing a set of jagged, incredibly sharp teeth. Teeth that were surely present in order to aid the dinosaur in its consumption of meat. Teeth that were perfectly designed for the tearing and ripping of flesh. Jacob imagined one of those teeth sinking effortlessly into his arm. He shuddered.

"Dexter," Jacob whispered, trying not to move his mouth. "Is that an allosaurus?"

"No," Dexter whispered. "It's a torvosaurus. It's *bigger* than an allosaurus."

"Let's get out of here," Sarah whispered.

Jacob took out the time machine and nodded. Sarah and Dexter reached out and grabbed his hand.

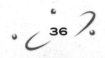

"May second, 2012, clearing in the forest, seven p.m. One, two . . ."

"Wait!" Sarah whispered furiously. "Where's Chloe?"

Jacob whipped his head around. Chloe was nowhere to be seen.

Just as his mind registered her disappearance, the torvosaurus charged out of the forest.

"We have to get out of here!" Jacob shouted.

"Not without Chloe!" Sarah hissed frantically. "Where is she?!"

The torvosaurus was bounding toward them. Jacob was about to say "Warp" as a simple matter of survival when the small, very uninteresting othnielia started running toward the giant carnivore. Jacob couldn't imagine what its tiny reptilian brain was thinking. It was only three feet tall, maybe, and it was heading straight toward a thirty-five-foot killing machine.

Jacob thought he saw the torvosaurus's eyes glint as it saw the othnielia approach. It opened its jaws and lowered its massive head down for a chomp, but the othnielia darted to the side and ran straight through the torvosaurus's legs. The torvosaurus made one last lunge through its hind legs to catch the little reptile, tripped over its own head, and collapsed in an earth-shaking heap.

"Whoa," Dexter said. "Go, othnielia."

The torvosaurus regained its composure and went bounding off into the forest after the othnielia.

They were safe. For the moment.

"Y ou people are crazy," Chloe said when she emerged from the bushes a few moments later. "I can't believe you were going to just stand there and get eaten."

Jacob reached for Sarah. "No, don't—"

He was too late.

Sarah Daisy lunged at her sister and tackled her into the dirt. She pinned Chloe's shoulders to the ground with her knees and pointed a finger in her face.

"Don't you ever scare me like that again!" Sarah yelled.

Chloe laughed, which Jacob knew would make Sarah only angrier. He ran over and pulled Sarah off her sister and held her back, surprised as always at how powerful she was when she had a full head of steam. After a few moments he finally felt her relax a bit and he released her.

She stomped away to regain her composure.

Jacob turned back to Chloe, trying to keep a calm voice. "Chloe, if we're ever in danger again, you really need to come over to the time machine and—"

"Blah, blah, blah," Chloe said. "You're not the king of the jungle, Jacob Wonderbar."

Jacob wondered if the torvosaurus might still be hungry.

He turned his back on her, marveling that she had managed to top the time she dumped a bucket of water on Sarah and Jacob from the upstairs window when they were about to hug good night. Or kiss good night, Jacob briefly thought before pushing the idea out of his mind.

Sarah rejoined the circle with her hands stuffed in her pockets, though Jacob noticed she was still so angry, she was unable to look at Chloe. "Let's get her back to the present." She jutted out her jaw. "Whether she wants to go or not."

"But wait," Jacob said. "If Chloe came from the future, we should take her back to *her* present time. Chloe, what day is it for you?"

Jacob knew he had to get her back to whatever day she had traveled back in time. If they brought her back

to the present and she hadn't gone back in time yet, there would be two Chloes at the same time, and Jacob was quite sure he could not handle that.

Chloe pouted for a moment, then smiled. "It's the eleventy-fifth of Octember," she said with a sarcastic flip of her hair.

Jacob could feel the blood pounding in his temples. "Forget it," he said. "We'll just take her back to our time."

"But then there will be two of her running around!" Sarah shouted. "Think about it, Jacob, what are we going to do with this The Brat *and* past The Brat? It's bad enough dealing with one of her."

"I can hear you!" Chloe said.

Jacob sighed and turned back to Chloe. "Listen," Jacob said, trying to keep his voice as even as possible. "We really need to get you back to the correct time. Would you, pretty please, tell us what day we need to take you back to?"

Chloe crossed her arms and squinted at Jacob. "Fine," she said. "I'll tell you."

Jacob waited as patiently as he could manage.

"It's the thirty-twelfth of Marchuary." She leaned her head back and cackled.

Jacob grabbed her hand. "That's it. We're leaving."

Dexter grabbed Chloe's hand as well. She beamed

at him, but he was looking off into the forest, his face bright red. Sarah stood in place for a moment before reluctantly taking Jacob's hand.

"Okay, here we go," Jacob said. "My house, noon, May *sixteenth,* 2012. Warp!"

Jacob felt a prick on his leg when he said "warp," and the air rushed out of his chest. When he opened his eyes, he enjoyed the thoroughly surprised look on Chloe's face. He had tricked her. He just had a hunch that two weeks into the future was the correct time.

"Lucky guess?" Jacob smirked.

Then he saw the real reason Chloe looked so surprised.

The othnielia took off running down the street.

Chapter 10

Nelly!" Dexter shouted. "Nelllyyyyyyy!!!"

Jacob Wonderbar sat on the curb near the forest with his arms crossed, trying to clear his frustrated brain. He didn't know where to find his dad. He didn't know why he had run into Sarah Daisy's kid sister in the Jurassic era. And he had just unleashed a several-hundred-million-year-old dinosaur on his unsuspecting neighborhood.

The only consolation was that at least it was the othnielia and not the torvosaurus.

Sarah stared at the forest and shook her head. "Jake, even if we *see* that thing, how are we going to catch it?"

Chloe cackled. "You guys are so busted."

Sarah whipped her head around at her sister and

jabbed a finger past Chloe's ear in the direction of their house.

"Go home."

Chloe smiled and said, "I don't think Dexter—"

"Go. Home," Sarah said.

Chloe kept on smiling at Sarah before she suddenly twirled around twice and started walking very slowly in the direction of her house. Then she stopped and turned around, staring with a venom that caught Jacob by surprise. He wondered if they should be keeping an eye on her after all.

"You'll regret this," she said icily.

"I don't think we will," Sarah shot back. "Go home."

"Nelly! Nellllyyyyyyy!" Dexter shouted, before noticing Chloe walking away. "Oh. Bye, Chloe."

She turned her head up and smiled at Dexter as she walked away.

Jacob muttered, "Now what?"

It was time to think of a plan. They had squandered enough time looking for dinosaurs and dealing with Chloe. But Jacob felt so confused.

His dad was in Milwaukee or in outer space or lost in time or who knew where. He didn't know where to find him, he didn't even know if his dad wanted to be found, and Jacob was tired just thinking about how long he had worried about his dad and what he was doing.

He was tired of being the one doing the looking.

"Maybe I should just go back and talk to my dad when he used to live at home. To see if he knows anything," Jacob said.

"Do you think that will work?" Sarah asked. "I mean, if someone is lost, does it work to ask them beforehand where they're going to lose themselves?"

"So how do you find someone who's lost?" Jacob asked.

Sarah tapped her fingers together softly. "Maybe we need to make him come to us. You know how when people are missing in the forest they make a huge fire so the rescuers can find them? What about something like that, only with time? Something really big."

"Nellyyyy!" Dexter shouted.

Nelly shot out of the brush and ran in front of a passing car. Dexter shrieked, but the car swerved at the last second, nearly hit a fire hydrant, and honked angrily as it passed.

Nelly stopped, perched on the curb, and stared at Jacob, Dexter, and Sarah for a moment. Then he took off running down the street again.

Dexter smacked his face. "That thing is a menace."

"What do you think?" Sarah asked. She reached

out and gently pushed Jacob's head to the side and it made him smile.

"You're right. We need to make history," he said. "Major history. So my dad will know where we are in time and have to come find us."

Sarah's eyes glinted. "You have an appointment with Phil this afternoon, right?"

Jacob did some quick calculations. "Yeah, I guess it's Wednesday."

"I have an idea," she said.

Chapter 11

Tell me about your feelings," Phil the therapist said.

Jacob Wonderbar was sitting on what had to be the most comfortable couch on the Planet Earth. He sunk into the plush, cool cushions, slowly rested his head back, and felt his eyelids lower in pleasure. He knew those cushions were really a secret weapon to make him feel calm enough to spill his guts, but they were so cozy, he wasn't sure he cared. Every Wednesday afternoon he settled into this couch for a chat with Phil and tried not to fall asleep.

Dexter was busy thumbing through a thick book on Carl Jung.

"I'm pleased you brought your friends today," Phil said. "Perhaps we can all learn together."

Jacob badly wanted Sarah's plan to work. It was so simple and logical. They had no idea what year Jacob's dad had been lost in time, so it made sense to go far back in history and make something big happen. If someone had just gone back to teach cavemen the principles of conflict resolution, and if early humans had learned to solve their differences in a calm and rational fashion, then maybe there would never have been such a thing as war. What could possibly be bigger than that? And if war had never been invented, not only would the world be a wildly better place, but the Timekeeper, the person responsible for tracking unauthorized time travel, would notice the massive difference in history no matter what year he was stranded in.

He'd have to trace it back to the source: Phil. Since Jacob's dad had been friends with Phil before he moved away, it wouldn't take much to realize Jacob had a time machine and needed to be found.

They would change the entire course of history. With a very polite therapist.

"Do you believe in nonviolence?" Sarah asked.

Phil cocked his head and gently tapped his fingertips together in front of his face. He had short gray hair and long gray nose hairs.

"Do *you* believe in nonviolence?" Phil asked reasonably.

"Yes," Sarah said. "Well . . . I try."

Phil nodded as if he expected her to say that, then he settled back in his chair and stared at Sarah. She stared back in confusion.

"And?" she asked. "What about you?"

Phil was silent.

Jacob raised his eyelids long enough to say to Sarah, "This is the part where he waits for you to say something. It's his favorite trick. He'll stay like that for an hour until you talk about your parents."

"Say something," Sarah said.

Phil stretched his shoulder slightly but stayed silent.

"Say something!" Sarah yelled.

Phil sniffed and scratched a note on his pad.

"What are you writing?" Sarah asked. "What are you saying about me?"

Phil smiled, clicked his pen closed, and folded his hands with a benevolent smile.

"Boogaloo!" Sarah waved her hands.

Phil's expression didn't change.

"Did you know that not talking is a sign of insanity?" Sarah asked. She crossed her arms and squinted at him and waited for a full minute. Phil still refused to speak.

Sarah nodded to Jacob. "He's perfect," she said.

Jacob peeled himself off of the couch and waved to

Dexter, who gave him a thumbs-up. They all ran and grabbed Phil, who nearly fell backward in his chair in surprise.

"The Great Rift Valley, two hundred thousand years ago, one p.m., warp!" Jacob shouted.

Chapter 12

Tell me about your feelings," Phil said to the caveman. "What are you feeling right now?"

"Oo!" the caveman shouted. He scratched his long, tangled beard. He was wearing nothing but some scrappy animal furs that looked like they hadn't been washed in a while. If ever.

They had stumbled upon the caveman after spotting a wisp of smoke over the savannah, and apparently they had found themselves an exceedingly calm caveman, because he didn't even run away when they approached. He just pointed at them, waved happily, and said "Oo!" and didn't otherwise move an inch. Jacob wondered if he was able to stay calm because he had a massive club resting on the ground next to him and looked strong enough to bash them all to bits.

Jacob stared at a small beast roasting on a spit for a moment before saying "Oo!" to the caveman, who nodded happily and said "Oo!" back.

"Tell me everything," Phil said in his best reassuring voice. "What is your family situation like?"

Jacob didn't have the heart to remind Phil that the caveman did not speak English, as it had not been invented yet.

"The caveman smells," Dexter said.

"Shh!" Sarah said.

"I want you to take a deep breath and just really focus on your physical sensations," Phil said, undeterred. "Can you do that for me? Let your mind expand into the open space around you. Feel yourself in your own skin, then let your mind move into the space beyond your skin. Just let everything wander and then tell me how you feel."

The caveman pointed at Phil's silver wristwatch. "Eck!"

"Watch," Phil said, pointing.

"Wetch," the caveman said.

"Whoa!" Dexter said. "He almost said a word!"

"He's not an idiot," Sarah said.

"Eedot," the caveman said, looking at Sarah with wide eyes. "Eedot! Eedot! Eedot!"

The children were silent for a moment.

"Eedot!" the caveman grabbed his club, stood up, and pounded the ground several times. Then he turned to the children and smiled happily. "Eedot."

"How does that word make you feel?" Phil asked.

The caveman stared at Phil for a while. "Oo!" he said finally.

Jacob stood up. He'd seen enough of Phil's attempt at conflict resolution to know that it was going to take an extremely long time.

"Sarah, Dexter, could I have a word?" Jacob asked.

Sarah and Dexter followed him a short way away, and they sat down on a rough log. Jacob batted at some extremely large flies that looked very eager to feast on one of his arteries.

"We have to ditch Phil," Jacob said.

"What?!" Sarah whispered. "We can't just *leave* him here."

They looked over at the campfire. Phil was placing his watch on Eedot's wrist. Eedot trembled in excitement.

Jacob turned back to Sarah and Dexter. "He'll be fine. We can always come back here and pick him up later. Phil's job could take an entire lifetime. He's going to have to start with Eedot and educate a whole bunch more people. He's probably going to have to learn their language too."

Dexter scratched his chin. "I guess there's not that much harm. If something happens to him, we can come back and reverse it."

"Exactly," Jacob said.

Sarah raised a finger. "But where are we going to—"

"EEDOT!" Eedot shouted from right behind them.

"Ah!!" Dexter shouted as he fell backward over the log.

"Eedot?" Eedot whispered in concern, bending over to stare at Dexter. He pointed at Phil's watch and beamed.

Dexter hopped up and scrambled over to Jacob. "Let's go," he said. "Phil can handle this."

Jacob had an idea. He'd almost forgotten he still had his Astral Telly, the outer space version of a cell phone. "Hey Phil," he shouted. "If you see my dad, tell him to go to May sixteenth, 2012, and call me on my Telly."

Phil looked confused by what Jacob had just said, but he was quickly distracted when Eedot presented him with a dead animal in return for the watch.

Jacob took out the key. They wandered into some scrubby bushes so Eedot and Phil wouldn't see them disappear. When they were safely out of view, Sarah and Dexter grabbed on to the time machine and Jacob said, "May sixteenth, 2012, my house, one p.m. . . ."

Just before Jacob said "Warp," he noticed Dexter out of the corner of his eye look down, loosen his grip on the key, and say, "What the . . ."

Jacob said "Warp" and felt his stomach drop and the air rush out of his lungs, and when he opened his eyes, he was staring at his house. Only it was overgrown with dark green ivy. He stared down his street, which wasn't a street at all but an idyllic creek surrounded by tall trees. Wooden pods attached to stiff vines sped high through the trees, carrying people down the street. The sidewalks were peaceful dirt paths. Jacob could hear birds chirping loudly and insects buzzing through the treetops. The street where all the houses looked the same had transformed into a verdant paradise.

"Where are we?" Jacob said.

"Um," Sarah said, looking around in a panic. "More importantly, where is Dexter?"

Chapter 13

Jacob stared at the computer for more than thirty seconds. It was so disgusting, he wasn't sure he could touch it.

"That's the computer?" he asked the librarian.

"Young man, don't tell me you've never seen a computer before!" the librarian tittered before shuffling away. "May your emotions be calm and your mind clear," she called over her shoulder.

Jacob's eyes widened and he nudged Sarah. "That's what Phil always says."

"Jake . . ." Sarah said, pointing at the desk.

The computer was breathing. It was the size of an old desktop computer, but the monitor was covered in flesh and its screen glistened like a giant eyeball. The keyboard looked sweaty, and instead of plastic buttons, the keys looked like overgrown goose bumps. Jacob sat down in the chair and wondered if he should ask the computer permission before he touched it.

"Do you think it's alive?" Jacob asked.

"It's definitely alive," Sarah said. "The question is whether it has teeth."

Jacob gulped. He didn't relish the idea of being bitten by a living computer.

Jacob took a deep breath. "I'm just going to . . ."

The computer burped.

Jacob smacked his head. "Seriously?"

"Hurry, Jake," Sarah said, staring at a thorny plant nearby, which was slowly turning in their direction. "I think the plants are getting restless."

When he opened up the browser a headline in large block letters read: "Rumors of Dinosaur Sightings Terrify Local Neighborhood." A bit farther down, another headline said: "Area Man Claims to be President of the Universe, Wins Steak-Eating Competition."

Jacob's hands paused over the keyboard. "Uh-oh."

They would have to deal with Nelly and Old Mick later. First he had to find Dexter. He carefully tapped the letter G.

The computer exhaled in pleasure. Jacob shivered and kept going. At least it didn't seem hostile.

Jacob found Google, which, thankfully still existed in whatever alternate reality Jacob and Sarah had landed themselves in. He entered "Dexter Goldstein," but then paused before pressing ENTER.

He turned to Sarah. "What if the future is different because sending Phil back worked? Do you think my dad will find us?"

Sarah looked away, knowing she needed to tread carefully whenever Jacob's father was the subject of the conversation.

Jacob glanced at his Telly. No missed calls. He felt a queasy stirring in his stomach, feeling somewhat crazy that he was thinking it was possible that he would call.

His dad almost felt imaginary, an impossible phantom he was chasing that always seemed just out of reach.

His heart sank yet again.

Sarah squeezed his shoulder. "Let's find Dexter."

Jacob nodded. He hit ENTER and scrolled through the results. The computer sighed and said, "Good choice, flesh being."

"Um. Thanks," Jacob said. He hoped the computer wouldn't try to make conversation.

The first result that Jacob found was "Le Boulevard de Dexter Goldstein," which was in Paris.

"Maybe he ended up in France?"

The second result was for the artist Jacques-Louis David. Jacob clicked on it and saw a lavish painting of a coronation scene inside a grand cathedral. The king was placing a crown on his queen's head, and all of the various heads of state and dukes and duchesses were standing around in their finest attire. While everyone else in the painting appeared quite serious, Dexter was standing next to the king, smiling and giving a thumbs-up.

"That's Dexter!" Jacob shouted. "What is he doing with a king?!"

"May I interest you in a beverage?" the computer asked. "Some gear grease, perhaps?"

"No," Jacob said quickly. Then he remembered that the computer might have teeth. "I mean, no thank you, kind computer sir."

He clicked back to the previous screen and started looking for a historical article. Surely there had to be more information about Dexter if he had wound up in a famous painting. Next to a king. At least a couple hundred years ago.

Then he felt Sarah's hand on his shoulder.

"Jake, that wasn't just a king," she whispered. "That was Napoleon Bonaparte."

Chapter 14

"Notre Dame Cathedral, Paris, December . . ."

Sarah laughed. "No, Jake, it's not pronounced like the football team, it's 'No-truh dahm.' It's French."

"Oh. Notre Dame Cathedral, Paris, December second, 1804, eleven a.m., warp!"

Jacob closed his eyes, he felt the air rush out of his lungs, and in front of him was Notre Dame Cathedral. It was one of the most spectacular places he had ever seen. Two magnificent white towers rose up above grand arched doorways, which were topped with an eerie row of dozens of beheaded statues. The towers were streaked with black soot, but it only made the cathedral more imposing and beautiful at the same time. Old wooden buildings were built right up to the cathedral's entrance, which forced Jacob to tip his head back and stare straight up to see the tops of the towers.

Jacob and Sarah found themselves at the edge of an excited crowd that was jostling and shoving for a better view. A row of finely dressed guards armed with muskets and shiny bayonets were keeping the crowd at bay. Jacob could see his breath in the cold December air and rubbed his arms for warmth.

"We have to get inside," Sarah said.

Jacob felt a push from behind and found his face within a few inches of a bayonet, which was held by a stern bearded soldier who looked as if he would not mind impaling a twelve-year-old. Jacob ducked back before the crowd could push him again.

He grabbed Sarah's hand for safety, but she pulled away from him.

"I can take care of myself, thank you very much," she said.

"Ugh. Fine," Jacob said.

They started worming their way through the frenzied throng toward the side of the cathedral. Suddenly the crowd gasped, and Jacob looked up into the sky to see a massive balloon lit with hundreds of lights lifting into the sky. He looked away quickly and

used the distraction to make a final push to the side of Notre Dame. He spotted a small door, which was down some stairs and almost hidden at the base of the cathedral. Jacob thought it must surely lead to the inside. It was guarded by a very tall and very muscular guard, whose jaw jutted out in a rather intimidating fashion.

Jacob and Sarah stared up at the guard. The guard stared down at them. Jacob knew he needed a good distraction.

"Excuse me," Jacob said. "Can you please tell me how to get to the Eiffel Tower?"

Sarah smacked her head. "Jake," she whispered. "The Eiffel Tower doesn't exist yet."

"*Des enfants anglais?*" the guard said, alarmed. "*Á Paris?*"

"Um. I'm not an infant." Jacob said.

"*Enfant* means 'child,'" Sarah whispered.

The soldier shouted "*Des espions anglais!*" and pointed at the children, but luckily the crowd was still buzzing with excitement and his comrades didn't hear him.

Jacob quickly turned to Sarah, whose face had gone ashen. "What does that mean?"

"Spies," she whispered. "He thinks we're English spies!"

The guard stepped carefully toward them. A

beautiful hymn started playing within the cathedral and the crowd outside shushed each other so they could hear what was happening. The guard took a deep breath to shout again, so Jacob did the only thing he could think to do. He charged straight into the guard's belly.

Jacob's impact stifled the guard's shout and he tripped over his decorative cape as he stumbled back. He landed with an "oomph" against the wall of the cathedral, and the sound drew the attention of two nearby soldiers, who yelped in alarm and started running toward them.

Jacob threw the small door open and saw a tiny staircase. He started running up, with Sarah close behind.

Around and around Jacob went up the stone spiral staircase. His chest started burning after it seemed like they had climbed for an eternity, but whenever his legs wanted him to slow down, all he needed to hear were the shouts and footsteps of the soldiers chasing him to keep climbing.

Finally he reached a door and he pushed it open and ran back out into the cold. They were on a stone ledge midway up the tower, and all of smoky, ramshackle Paris spread out before them. He could see the spires of old churches and the river Seine and the tops of ancient wooden buildings and the crowd below.

Just as they arrived, Jacob and Sarah heard a soldier yell *"Halte!"* and they ran along a narrow ledge in between the towers and ducked into another small door. Jacob looked up at a massive bell, which he hoped would not ring while they were inside. The classical music from the coronation wafted up into the tower, and Jacob tried to peer down to see if he could catch a glimpse of Dexter.

He didn't see Dexter, but he did see a ladder that stretched down in between the wooden belfry and the stone side of the cathedral.

He scrambled over and started climbing down, the wood rickety and creaking underneath his weight. He peeked down at the floor, which was far, far below. He swallowed against his dry throat. He needed to focus.

After dozens of rungs he dropped down into a gallery near the rear of the cathedral. Sarah was right behind him. Jacob risked a glance through organ pipes to see the coronation in progress. Hundreds of men and women dressed in gold and red and deep purple were standing serenely watching the proceedings. The inside of the cathedral was lit by elaborate candelabras, and the ceilings were hung with banners and tapestries. Jacob knew that Dexter was probably somewhere near the front of the church, which was so far away, he could barely see it.

Jacob heard a grunt above, and looked up to see one of the grim soldiers peering down at him. He knew they wouldn't risk causing a commotion by shouting, and Jacob rushed through a doorway and down another spiral staircase.

They reached the ground floor and suddenly they were among the most important people in France and around Europe, the generals and dukes and statesmen, wearing their finest clothes and hats. The women were dressed in flowing dresses and wore tiaras and sparkling jewels in their hair.

Jacob and Sarah gave each other a quick glance and started running up the aisle of the cathedral toward the front. Behind them they heard a growing clamor as the confused spectators wondered why two strangely dressed children were interrupting Napoleon's coronation. The murmurs soon turned to shouts. Jacob hoped no one would stop them.

As they neared the front of the cathedral, Jacob caught a glimpse of Napoleon, a short man with a large nose who looked increasingly angry the closer they got.

Two of Napoleon's personal guards started marching toward the children, but after a quick, testy order from Napoleon, they sheepishly retreated.

Instead Napoleon clutched a massive golden scepter and patted it in his hand in anticipation.

Jacob tried to look around as he ran, but there was no sign of Dexter. Napoleon shrugged off his red cape, yelled *"Assassins!"* and started marching menacingly toward Jacob and Sarah, waving his scepter.

Jacob stopped in his tracks and held up his hands. He didn't need a translator to know what Napoleon had just said. Strong men grasped Jacob's shoulders. Napoleon raised the scepter.

"Non!" Jacob heard a familiar voice shout.

Dexter, dressed in a fine gold coat, blue knickers, and crisp white stockings, stepped in front of Jacob and Sarah.

"Ce sont mes amis," Dexter said.

"They're my friends," Sarah whispered, exhaling in relief.

Chapter 15

Jacob strolled with Sarah and Dexter through the Jardin des Tuileries, a beautiful garden where Parisians of all types tried to soak in some sun in the short December afternoon. The garden was filled with intricate topiaries cut into the shapes of large animals, and many different types of trees, and it reminded Jacob of the king's garden back on Planet Royale.

Dexter was still wearing his fine embroidered gold coat, and seemed even taller than Jacob had remembered. A sullen soldier with a musket trailed behind them for protection. Jacob was thankful the soldier was there, because the Parisians couldn't stop staring at his sneakers.

"So I said to Bonnie," Dexter continued, his voice sounding just a bit lower than normal. Jacob wondered if he had a cold. "Oh, I call him Bonnie because his last name is Bonaparte, get it? I said to Bonnie, 'No way man, you don't want to go to war with England'—he's obsessed with invading England, I don't really understand why, there hasn't been a war in thousands of years—'Let me tell you about this thing called recycling.' He loved it! Bonnie is a really great general and everything, but he just needed something else to excite his natural curiosity. He converted to Philism and got really into gardening. He started turning all the extra cannons and muskets into better sewer pipes, which sounds gross, but it made things a lot better around here. Oh! Remember Phil the therapist? He's huge! When people want to say hi to each other here they say *'Dites-moi ce que vous ressentez.'* It means 'Tell me about your feelings.'"

"Wow," Jacob said.

"I know!" Dexter said. "Go, Phil."

Sarah smacked Jacob on the shoulder. "That's why our town was like a forest! Napoleon must have started environmentalism early and people made biological machines instead of plastic, and it changed the way people built cities!"

Jacob felt the key in his pocket and knew they had succeeded in wildly changing the course of history. Phil had left his mark and even Dexter the Great

Recycler had managed to stop Napoleon's famous invasions.

So where was his dad? Surely the Timekeeper would have noticed the massive disruptions in the course of history. Jacob's heart began to sink. Yet another plan to find his father had failed. Even completely altering world history hadn't worked.

"How long have you been here?" Jacob asked.

"About a year."

"I thought you looked taller!" Sarah said.

Dexter looked down at Jacob. "Whoa. I am now your elder."

"It's weird," Jacob said. "Should we go back to the day you were sent back in time to France and pick you up so you'll be the same age again?"

"I kind of like being taller than you." Dexter smiled.

Jacob stood up straighter. "Who stranded you here, anyway?" Jacob asked.

"I don't know," Dexter said. "Someone grabbed my foot when we were warping away in Africa and the next thing I knew I was in France. I never got a good look at who it was."

Dexter suddenly remembered something and stopped in his tracks.

"Guys, they know about Astrals," Dexter said quietly.

"What?!" Sarah shrieked.

"Who? The French? How do you know?" Jacob asked.

Dexter ushered them over next to a tree and quickly glanced around to see if anyone was watching. Jacob figured the precaution was probably rather unnecessary, as no one he had met in 1804 France spoke English. But he didn't want to interrupt Dexter's story.

"So I was wandering around the palace one night looking at all the tapestries. They're really creepy because the eyes follow you and when you walk around by candlelight, it's kind of scary even though it's just woven fabric and I'm trying to be more—"

"Dex, Astrals . . ." Sarah said.

"Oh, right. So I found this one tapestry in the basement of the palace. It was one of the oldest ones in the entire palace, from ancient times, and it was completely faded. The only reason I even found it was because Bonnie gave me the key to the basement so that I could protect the seeds for his favorite types of flowers, which are really valuable here because it's 1804 and when you want a new plant, you can't just go down to the florist and pick up a—"

"Okay, so you found an old tapestry . . ." Jacob said.

Dexter's eyes were wide. "Guys. It had a spaceship on it."

"What?" Jacob asked.

"Shut up," Sarah said. "No way."

"I swear," Dexter said. "And it had the Crackenarium family seal on it. It's not even science fiction. It's the real thing."

Jacob's mind raced. They knew about Astrals in ancient times? How did it never make the history books?

"It gets worse," Dexter said, interrupting Jacob's thoughts. "I think there's a secret society to destroy space humans."

Chapter 16

"But that was a long time ago, right?" Sarah said. "Surely there's no one trying to destroy Astrals in our time."

Sarah and Jacob and Dexter stared at the tapestry in the basement of the Palais des Tuileries, Napoleon's personal palace. There was no mistaking the authenticity of the spaceship it depicted. It looked like an earlier model of the spaceship Praiseworthy, with slightly rougher edges and far less impressive rocket boosters. More importantly, it most definitely sported the Crackenarium seal. Jacob tried to work through what it meant. Humans on Earth knew about Astrals a really long time ago. But how many knew?

Napoleon burped. He was sitting in the corner in a big red chair wearing a full military uniform with hundreds of medals. He said *"Je vous prie de m'excuser"* without looking up from his huge book on flowers.

Jacob looked around the rest of the basement, which was full of ancient wood cabinets, magnificent rows of books, and strange exotic plants that Dexter was protecting from the chilly weather outside. They were arranged carefully near a huge fireplace where a large log burned, radiating warmth throughout the room. Hanging in the center of the ceiling was an ornate chandelier with dozens of candles that dripped wax into a sticky pool on the floor.

"Think about it," Dexter said. "Astrals were always so worried about Earth and how we were going to war with them, accusing us of being spies and all that stuff about Earth being a menace. What if they weren't wrong? What if there was something to it and people from Earth really do want to destroy Astrals?"

"But it's just a tapestry." Sarah waved her hand at it dismissively. "Sure, now we know humans know about Astrals a long time ago, but how do you know that Earth is a danger to them?"

"Because I did more research," Dexter said. He walked over to a bookshelf and pulled out a massive leather-bound tome that was nearly three feet long and thousands of pages thick. He placed it on a rough wooden table. Jacob was impressed by Dexter's feat of

strength. There was no way he would have been able to lift something that big before.

Jacob stepped over to the book and opened it to its title page. He was surprised to see that it was written in English and not French. Its title was *On the Origin and Danger of Human Species Not Originating on Our Planet*.

He thumbed through the pages and saw intricate prints of spaceship encounters, diagrams of planets, extensive theories about the possible source of space humans, detailed accounts of Astral pranks, and what appeared to be a lengthy manifesto about the moral duty of exterminating them. Whoever had made the book had seemingly spent their entire life trying to compile every known fact about every possible encounter with people from outer space. And they certainly did not seem very nice about it.

Jacob supposed that it was natural that humans would have been scared of Astrals. After all, he remembered the exhibit he had seen on Planet Archimedes that showed a video of Astrals tipping over a woolly mammoth and terrifying some early humans. Astrals loved pranks, and how could they have resisted messing with Earthers? And people were often hostile toward things they were scared of.

But there was a big difference between being

suspicious and actually trying to destroy Astrals. Even as he thumbed through the strange book, Jacob was still skeptical that there was such a thing as a secret society on Earth that wanted to wipe out space humans.

"There's more," Dexter said. The light from the candles and fire danced across his face and made him seem even more serious than he sounded.

"When I first arrived in France, everyone was scared of me because I was wearing modern clothes and didn't speak French, so they took me to this weird group that wore black robes and necklaces with gold triangles. I didn't know what everyone was saying, but I think they thought I was an Astral. I thought they were going to kill me! They took me straight to Napoleon and there was a lot of arguing. Bonnie let me stay in the palace, which made all those scary people really mad. We hit it off right away, didn't we Bonnie?"

Napoleon looked confused. *"Je ne comprends pas ce que vous dites."*

"Je leur raconte comment nous nous sommes rencontrés," Dexter said.

"Ce fut un plaisir! Quelle histoire amusante!" Napoleon collapsed into fits of laughter. Dexter joined in and they high-fived.

"See?" Dexter said to Jacob. "It was hilarious."

"Um, right. Who were the scary people?" Jacob asked.

"Oh, yeah. Bonnie would never say, even after I learned French. But I think they were a secret anti-Astral society."

"Wait a second," Sarah said. "Dex, isn't it strange that you just happened to find all of this Astral stuff out from meeting Napoleon Bonaparte? What happened to you after we met Eedot? Who could have sent you back in time into France?"

"Who do you think?" a very satisfied voice said from behind a bookshelf.

"*Sacrebleu!*" Napoleon shouted. "*Qui êtes-vous?*"

Mick Cracken, the twelve-year-old Mick Cracken, former prince and current president of the universe, stepped into the center of the room and greeted them with an insufferable gloating grin. He clapped his hands together in silent self-congratulation.

"You . . ." is all Jacob managed to say.

"I think you mean 'Hello, Mr. President,'" Mick said.

Jacob and Sarah and Dexter looked around at one another and shook their heads. Of course it was Mick Cracken.

Mick reached into his pocket and held up a golden key. "What? Did you really think I'd let you have my only time machine?"

Chapter 17

What are you doing here?" Jacob asked, glaring at Mick.

Mick smiled. "All in due time, all in due time . . . First I have to memorize the expression on your faces right now so I can savor it for the rest of my life."

"Ugh. Forget it. Let's get out of here," Jacob said, taking the time machine out of his pocket. "Before he can send one of us back to the Dark Ages."

Jacob was furious that Mick was interfering yet again. He had marooned Jacob and Dexter on Numonia, he had sent kidnappers after Jacob when he had tried to run for president of the universe, and now he'd stranded Dexter in revolutionary France. Whatever peace Jacob had made with Mick after the election completely evaporated.

"Before you go . . ." Mick said. He looked completely relaxed, as if there were no reason at all that Jacob, Sarah, and Dexter would be mad at him. He looked as if he may as well have been hosting a tea party on Planet Royale. "Don't you want to talk about how we should work together?"

"Why would we work with you?" Sarah asked. "Dexter could have been killed."

Mick shook his head as if he were extremely disappointed by the collective intelligence on display.

"Let me ask you a question," Mick said, arching an eyebrow. "If I had told you that Astrals were in danger because of an Earther secret society, would you have believed me?"

Jacob and Dexter and Sarah looked around at one another. They all knew the answer was no, but none of them were willing to give Mick the satisfaction of admitting it. If Dexter hadn't seen the strange anti-Astral group and if Jacob hadn't leafed through the scary book, they wouldn't have believed that very many people on Earth had even heard of Astrals.

"That's what I thought," Mick said, rubbing his fingernails on his jacket. "Besides, I'm told Paris is a lovely city to visit in the fall."

"Not in 1804," Dexter said. "They don't have toilets. Thanks a lot, Cracken."

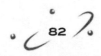

They heard a crash upstairs followed by some shouting.

"What was that?" Jacob asked.

Dexter's bodyguard charged into the room.

"Monsieur Goldstein! Vous êtes en danger. Ce sont les gens bizarres." He grasped his musket tightly and ran back upstairs.

"Les gens bizarres?!" Napoleon exclaimed. *"Ici? C'est scandaleux!"*

Sarah gasped. Dexter's face was white as he rushed over to lock the door. Jacob and Mick glanced at each other, uncomprehending.

"What did they say?" Jacob asked.

"It's the strange people," Dexter said. "They're back."

"And we're all in danger," Sarah added.

Jacob took out the time machine. "Let's go," he said. Dexter and Sarah rushed over to him and grabbed his shoulder.

He held up the key. "Present time, my house—"

"Before you go . . ." Mick said, his voice still calm despite the threat of imminent danger. He held up his golden key and examined the way it reflected the candles and the fire. "Wonderbar, I think you should come with me."

Jacob would have laughed if the situation didn't seem so urgent. "And why would I do that?"

Mick's eyes glinted. "I can help you find your father."

Sarah and Dexter whipped their heads around to see what Jacob thought. Jacob's heart raced and he stared straight back at Mick, unsure whether he was about to be trapped. Mick was a master of tricks, and Jacob knew he needed to tread carefully.

"How do you know where he is?" Jacob said, trying to keep his voice even.

Mick smiled. "Because I'm the one who sent him back in time."

A gunshot rang out in the hallway outside and the shouting became nearer and more desperate. There was urgent pounding on the door that soon turned into cracking. Someone was trying to batter the door open.

"It's them!" Dexter said.

"We have to get out of here!" Sarah shouted.

Jacob felt anger stirring within him. Mick acted as if sending Jacob's father back in time was the least interesting thing he had done that day. He seemed completely oblivious to the fact that Jacob might be upset about it. Instead, Mick simply held up his golden key and waited for Jacob to join him, as if it were a foregone conclusion that Jacob would believe him and follow him on whatever harebrained scheme Mick had concocted.

There was a smash at the door and the end of a long wooden log barreled through. The men outside pulled it back, and Jacob caught a glimpse of a man wearing a black hood, his faced scarred and twisted in anger. He wore a gold necklace with a triangle. Jacob had to make a decision.

He tossed his time machine to Sarah and Dexter. "I'll meet you back in the present," he said.

He grabbed on to Mick's time machine and braced himself for wherever Mick was going to take him.

"Wait!" Sarah shouted. She started running over to Jacob and he extended his hand.

She never reached him. Mick had already warped.

Chapter 18

Sarah sat down on the dirt path in front of her house on May 16, 2012, and slammed her hand down on a tuft of moss. An alarmed jackrabbit emerged from the bushes and ran away. Sarah tried to stop the angry tears that were welling in her eyes. Yet again, Jacob Wonderbar had gone charging off without her. He should have waited. He should have asked her what she thought he should do. They should have been a team.

They had been through so much in the past few weeks. It was almost as if they didn't have to talk anymore because they always knew what the other was thinking. Only now he had never felt so far away.

She stared at the stream trickling down the middle of the street where cars used to drive. Dexter sat down beside her. He patted her on the back.

"Hey," he said quietly. "Yeah."

She knew Dexter had no idea whatsoever what to say to make her feel better and that made her smile. He had clearly not become more eloquent after a year in France.

She thought about going on the scary living computer to see if she could locate Jacob, but somehow she figured Mick was too smart to leave a trail if he didn't want them to be discovered. She just hoped Jacob would return to them soon.

She took a steadying breath. "What do we do now, Dex?" Sarah asked.

"Um. How about first we figure out why our street looks like we landed in *The Lord of the Rings*?"

Sarah laughed. "Oh, right, I forgot you haven't seen it. We think it's because you taught Napoleon how to recycle."

Dexter looked around the neighborhood forest. "Hooray for me?"

Sarah heard a rustling behind her and she turned in time to see Nelly take a bite out of a pink flower. Nelly chewed quickly, paused, and stared at Sarah and Dexter with beady green eyes, and then took off running down the path.

Sarah buried her face in her hands. They really needed to get Nelly back to the Jurassic era. Of course,

as she looked around at her overgrown jungle of a neighborhood, she figured Nelly was feeling quite at home.

Sarah thought that she should go inside and see her parents and at least practice the piano or study for her Mandarin lesson, but she couldn't bear to go back home so soon after being ditched by Jacob. Being around her parents would just remind her of the fact that they didn't approve of him. They questioned whether he was a positive influence in her life, and it was only after intervention by Jacob's mother that Sarah was even allowed to see him after school.

They certainly wouldn't approve of her being upset over anything to do with Jacob Wonderbar. They might even sign her up for another extracurricular just so she had less time to spend with him.

Or even worse, they'd transfer her to another school. Sarah felt her anger returning. She didn't break rules and she loved her parents, but she didn't know why they couldn't see the real Jacob the way she could.

The door to Sarah's house flew open.

"Dexy!" she heard Chloe shout. "Dexy!" She started running toward the dirt path.

Dexter smiled, but Sarah knew Chloe better than he did. Chloe didn't sound excited, she sounded panicked.

"Happy . . . I mean . . . greetings," Dexter said as she approached.

Chloe reached them and looked down at Dexter. Her forehead was creased with worry.

"Dexy, it's your mom," Chloe said. "She's in the hospital."

Chapter 19

Where are you taking me?" Jacob asked.

Mick ignored Jacob and kept walking through the forest, glancing at his Telly and trampling through the bushes and branches that were in his way.

Jacob trailed behind Mick, keeping as close to him as possible just in case Mick tried to whip out his time machine and maroon Jacob in time, just as he had apparently done to Jacob's dad.

The forest was completely familiar—Jacob knew every root and shrub and stick in the scrubby little forest down the street from his house, the place where they had found the spaceship Lucy and where he had run from raccoons with Sarah and Dexter and where he spent many summer nights chasing fireflies and just being by himself.

But Jacob didn't know where they were in time.

"What year is it?" Jacob asked. Mick had whispered the destination when they warped and Jacob couldn't hear where they were going amid all the chaos at the Palace des Tuileries.

Mick didn't answer, didn't flinch, and didn't even turn around to acknowledge the question. Jacob stared at Mick's back, wondering for the hundredth time if he could really trust him. He had suspected from the beginning that Mick was somehow involved in his father's disappearance, as it had all the hallmarks of a Mick Cracken plot: nefarious actions, foul play, kidnapping, and making Jacob's life exceedingly difficult.

Mick was a master of deception and wouldn't think twice about using Jacob's father's predicament against Jacob.

But what was Mick trying to do? Why was he on Earth? And why would he try to help Jacob after he had previously marooned him on Numonia, sent crazed SEERs to try to kidnap him during the Astral presidential election, and generally treated Jacob as if he were his arch-nemesis?

Mick stopped and turned to face Jacob, giving him a wry smile. "You don't trust me," he said.

Jacob stared back at Mick and kept his face neutral. He would neither confirm nor deny.

Mick held up his hands. "I know we have a history. You have been my cleverest foe. But we're on the same side this time."

Jacob shook his head. "You're only on your own side."

Mick smiled happily. "You know me too well. But in this case my side happens to be your side."

"Then why did you ditch my dad in the past?"

Mick tapped a fist on his lips for a few moments in thought, then turned to walk away. "You'll see," he said over his shoulder.

Mick's nonchalance made Jacob's blood boil. Mick was messing with his father and acting as if it were the most natural thing in the universe. Jacob possessed so little trust in Mick, it was like the complete and total opposite of trust. Mick could spend the rest of his life telling nothing but the truth and being a perfect model citizen, and Jacob would still wonder if Mick was setting him up in some sort of long con game.

Jacob realized he needed to get control of the situation. He would steal Mick's time machine, warp back to the present, and leave Mick in the past until Jacob knew what to do with him. He would turn the tables.

He crept up behind Mick, who seemed lost in thought. Jacob crouched, ready to tackle Mick and wrest the key out of Mick's pocket.

Just as Jacob was ready to leap, Mick pointed at the ground and then craned his neck, looking around the forest, appearing very concerned.

Jacob stood up quickly and tried to read the expression on Mick's face. "What is it?"

"This is where and when I left your dad," Mick said. He gave Jacob a grim smile. "Only he's not here."

"But—" Before he could deal with Mick, Jacob's voice caught and he ducked down behind a bush.

Jacob saw a ten-year-old version of himself walk into the clearing.

Chapter 20

Dexter, Sarah, and Chloe huddled next to the door of Dexter's mom's hospital room. Doctors and patients streamed by. A tall nurse stopped and was about to speak to the children, most likely to ask them to move along, but one stern look from Sarah sent her on her way without a word.

Although the outside of the hospital was obscured by trees, the inside looked exactly like the hospital Dexter had long known and feared. Its shiny floors and white walls seemed designed solely to cause strange squeaky noises that inspired feelings of terror. He rubbed his hands over his face and avoided thinking about all of the fearsome medical devices in the general vicinity. He tried to breathe.

He had known something seemed off about his

mother. He had seen his parents having hushed conversations in the kitchen several different times. They would break off mid-sentence whenever he entered the room, giving him strange, pitying looks. But he had simply thought they were having money problems or were upset about his continued inability to avoid getting into trouble with Jacob Wonderbar. He had no idea it could have been something as serious as an illness.

Just then he saw his dad at the end of the hallway, and Dexter grabbed Sarah and Chloe and ducked around the corner. He hated to run away from his own father, but if his dad saw him, Dexter knew he would have to go into the hospital room and see his mom, and he wasn't sure if he could bear it.

They heard the door to the hospital room shut and edged closer so they could hear what was happening.

Dexter heard his mom say, "Have they found him?"

He almost felt like he could see her as she said it, her hair disheveled and staring up at the ceiling, worried . . . and then it hit him.

He *had* seen it, when he was on Planet Archimedes on his first space voyage, staring into the Looking Glass. When he had returned from space that time, he had expected to go home and find his mother sick, only she was fine.

But she wasn't fine after all. He realized that the scientists had shown him the future on Planet Archimedes.

"Sarah . . ." Dexter started to say.

Sarah nodded. "The Looking Glass. I just realized too." She hugged him and he squeezed out a tear when he clenched his eyes shut.

"What do you want to do?" Chloe asked.

Dexter thought about taking the time machine and zooming forward to the future to see what would happen. Maybe the illness was nothing and she would be fine and he wouldn't have to worry.

But he shuddered to think of the alternative. What if it were really bad? Then he would know and would have to go back and talk to his mom and say his goodbyes knowing full well what was going to happen. He couldn't do it.

It didn't feel real. His mom was a powerful individual, not someone who could be felled by something as small as a virus . . . or cancer.

But he remembered the time machine in Sarah's pocket. It didn't have to *be* real.

"Let's go into the past," Dexter whispered to Chloe and Sarah. "Let's fix this."

Sarah and Chloe glanced at each other. "But Dexy . . ." Chloe said.

"No," Dexter said, the strength in his voice surprising all three of them. "We have to. We have to make this better."

Sarah nodded slowly and took out the time machine. "Okay. We'll do it, Dex. Whatever you need. But what do you want to do?"

Dexter pointed at the key. "We'll go back in time and make her live a healthier lifestyle."

Chapter 21

Jacob watched the younger version of himself across the clearing. He was struck by how much smaller he was, just a kid who had no idea he would someday travel through space and time.

It was hard to watch his younger self plop down on a log, too numb to even cry. Younger Jacob looked so incredibly sad.

Jacob knew which day he was seeing. His dad had only moved away from home a few days before and young Jacob was having trouble believing it was really happening. He felt like he had woken up in someone else's life. He knew about things like divorce and kids who grew up with only one parent, and one of his classmates had no parents at all, but those were things that happened to other kids and on television

shows, not something that he had ever once thought could possibly happen to him. His life had completely changed overnight and there was nothing at all he could do about it.

His younger self slumped on the log, clutching a stick, too sad and bewildered to even hit anything with it. He just stared at the leaves and sat there.

Jacob recalled feeling like his whole body was on fire. He had been unable to pay attention to anything at school, he constantly tried to decide if he should tell people or not, and he wondered every day if things would ever feel normal again.

He had to completely change the way he thought about his life and the future. No more asking his dad first if he could spend the night at Dexter's because he'd be more likely to say yes than his mom. No more pancakes on Saturday mornings cut into strange shapes. No more surprise birthdays.

He was gone. And Jacob remembered this day in particular because it was the one where he started believing his dad really wasn't coming back.

"So . . ." Mick whispered.

Jacob shot him a look that made Mick back off. He wasn't leaving yet.

His younger self reached into his pocket and took out something small and green. Jacob remembered exactly what it was. Earlier that day, Sarah Daisy had rung the doorbell and pressed a flattened four-leaf clover into his hands with a sympathetic look. It was one of her most prized possessions and he took it wordlessly, knowing that he didn't have to say to her how much it meant to him.

The only reason he was able to get through the pain he felt when his dad left was because he had his friends and he had his mom, who cared about him and were patient with him when he wanted to talk

and when he didn't want to talk, and who didn't take it personally when he was mean to them for no reason other than that he was just angry. And he got through it, one slow, hard day at a time.

His younger self took out his cell phone and stood up to leave. Jacob remembered that his mom had texted him that dinner was ready. Little Jacob stomped away, and Jacob felt bad and happy for himself at the same time, knowing he had a long, hard road to go but that there was also so much happiness to look forward to.

Jacob glanced at Mick, who was twirling his finger, waiting for Jacob to say something.

And then it hit Jacob.

Mick had sent Jacob's dad back to this precise moment. He had tried to arrange a reunion.

exter, Sarah, and Chloe stood outside a brick
building covered in thick green ivy and waited
for Dexter's mom to emerge. The year was 1986, and
questionable fashion choices were everywhere.

There were men who had only one side of their
head shaved and wore a single thin earring. There
were women who apparently would not consider
wearing any article of clothing if it was not torn in
some manner. Men wore blazers over just a T-shirt.
Someone had decided that thick wool leggings around
the ankles were an appropriate accessory. And there
was a terrific race afoot to make one's hair as large
and as poufy as humanly possible.

Dexter noticed a particularly galling assemblage
of clothing. One woman wore a giant gray sweatshirt

that was ripped at the neck, exposing one shoulder, with jeans studded with rhinestones, purple leg warmers, and purple gloves with the fingers cut off. Then he realized he was staring at his mom.

"Whoa," Dexter said.

His jaw fell open and he pointed. Sarah and Chloe smiled and nodded, and they started trailing behind her a safe distance away.

Dexter struggled to take it all in. Her hair wasn't in a bun, it was all poofed out, a contender for the largest hairdo award. She didn't walk with purpose and efficiency, she . . . bounced. Happily. She wasn't someone who looked like she was overly concerned about beds being made and good grades achieved and a successful future secured; she looked like she did not have a thing to worry about in the universe.

Dexter looked at Sarah and Chloe. "I think my mom was cool," he whispered, hardly believing that those words were emerging from his mouth. His mom was fearsome, intensely caring, a force of nature, the smartest person he knew. But she most definitely was not cool.

"Ah!" Sarah shouted. She covered her mouth and pointed.

Dexter saw his mom saunter up to a tall blond

woman next to a tree. They started chatting casually.

"Ah!" he shouted, finally realizing who the blond woman was.

It was a younger Mrs. Daisy. Unlike Dexter's mom, Mrs. Daisy was dressed in a simple black sweater, jeans, and black boots, and she had forfeited the large hair competition. She was wearing librarian glasses and at age twenty or so, she looked eerily like a taller Sarah Daisy.

"Our moms were friends?" Sarah whispered.

"How is that possible?" Dexter asked.

And yet there was his mom, chatting with Mrs. Daisy, looking like the best of friends.

Sarah turned to Dexter, her eyes wide. "What happened to our parents?"

Dexter shook his head and looked at Chloe, who seemed oddly detached from everything they were seeing. But before he could attempt to formulate a coherent sentence to ask Chloe about why she didn't seem surprised, he saw his mom pull a small package out of her back pocket, shake it, take something out of it, and hand it over to Sarah's mom.

They were about to smoke a cigarette.

"No!" Dexter shouted.

"Mom!" Sarah gasped.

Their moms looked over at them, and it chilled Dexter to the bone when his mom's eyes just sort of glanced past him, not recognizing him.

Of course she didn't, he remembered. He wasn't born yet.

Dexter summoned his courage. Smoking was wrong. It was time for him to be the parent. He could save his mom from herself and maybe stop her from getting sick in the future.

He put his head down and charged over, and grabbed the cigarette out of his startled mom's hand. He stomped it on the ground and gave her a fierce look.

"You shouldn't smoke," he said.

He thought his mom was going to be furious at him like she was the few times he had ever dared talk back to her and defy her authority.

Instead she laughed, sounding surprisingly girlish, and patted him on his head. "Whatever," she said.

Sarah's mom tore her cigarette in half and Dexter's mom laughed at her.

"Shoo," Dexter's mom said, nudging him away.

Dexter slumped back to Sarah and Chloe.

"Okay, you did it, let's get back," Chloe said.

Dexter raised his head. "I'm not satisfied," he said in a low voice.

He spun around and followed his mom and Mrs. Daisy as they walked beside a boggy pond with large lily pads and croaking frogs. In an island at the center there was a rough sign with a painting of Phil the therapist's face that said: "Trust in Phil. Because your feelings are greater than gold."

They followed Dexter's mom to a hot dog stand, where she ordered a heaping chilidog covered in a strange yellow liquid cheese. Dexter shuddered. He had never seen his mom eat anything that wasn't made out of the healthiest and freshest ingredients. Who knows what consuming such a strange concoction could have done to her health. He started running.

"Go, Dex!" Sarah cheered.

Dexter ran up to his mom, smacked the chili cheese dog out of her hands, and yelled, "You should eat healthier food too!"

He kept running. The food splattered on the ground. Dexter looked over his shoulder expecting to see his mom exploding with rage.

She was laughing.

Chapter 23

What are you trying to do?" Jacob said, his voice strained.

Mick held up his hands, signaling for either time or calm, Jacob wasn't sure which. What Jacob did know was that he wasn't feeling calm and wasn't about to give Mick Cracken time to come up with a clever retort. Jacob balled his hands into fists and he wondered if he and Mick were going to have their first real fight.

"This is my life you're messing with," Jacob said. "My life. Not yours. Mine."

No one messed with Jacob Wonderbar. Not substitute teachers, not wannabe schoolyard bullies, not pretend space buccaneers who somehow got themselves elected president of the universe. And they certainly did not mess with his family. No matter how angry Jacob may have been with his father, he was *his* father, and Jacob would defend him until the end.

But Mick just stared back at Jacob, the first inklings of a satisfied grin beginning to form around the edges of his mouth.

Jacob felt a creeping thought in the back of his head and it slowed down his anger just a tad. He was still furious with Mick, but there was a small part of him that understood, maybe even appreciated, what Mick was trying to do. Jacob had spent endless afternoons wishing his dad would come home. He would go to bed dreaming of his dad being there in the morning making breakfast and destroying the kitchen in the process, or of showing up unannounced to one of his basketball games. And on that particular day when Jacob was ten years old and so sad sitting on the log, he would have given anything to see his father walk through the forest as a surprise visitor from the future.

What if Jacob's dad had shown up that day? What if his life had been different? What if Mick could have fixed Jacob's life and made it unfold the way it should have the first time around, with his dad still around day in and day out and surprising him with exciting presents on his birthday?

It almost seemed like Mick was trying to do the right thing for once, that the good side of Mick that seemed to hide just beneath his constant thievery and lying may finally have been emerging.

But he was still Mick Cracken. There had to be another angle. And Jacob realized he could have had the situation completely wrong.

Maybe Mick was dangling the idea of reuniting Jacob with his dad so he would follow Mick around for some other purpose. Maybe Mick was playing a bigger game and had no interest in helping Jacob find his dad at all. It could have all been one of Mick's patented tricks. He would make Jacob think he knew where his dad was so Jacob would trail along.

"What do you get out of this?" Jacob asked quietly.

Mick rubbed his chin and raised his eyebrows. "Why, Jacob Wonderbar, I would never presume to—"

"Spare me," Jacob said. "Did you really strand my dad in the past? Why would you even do that in the first place?!"

"Jacob," Mick said mock-patiently. "You have to understand—"

"All I understand is that you are a lying—"

"Listen," Mick said. He looked serious and sincere again.

"No, you listen to me . . ." Jacob said.

"Your dad is an Astral," Mick continued. "You're half Astral."

"I know that. So?"

"So Astrals are in danger, which means *you're* in danger. Think about it. There are life-changing things happening on your planet right now that could mean the end of all Astrals. Including you."

Jacob mulled over what Mick was saying, and ultimately found himself believing him. Jacob didn't have proof, but he felt like there was something brewing between Earth and Astrals. It made sense that Mick would find himself in the middle of it. Those strange people in the Palais des Tuileries certainly seemed scary, and Jacob believed that all Astrals could be in grave danger.

Mick's cocky smile returned in full force. "And I'm the only one who can save us. I have a plan."

Chapter 24

Dexter, Sarah, and Chloe stared at two male college students who wore fancy blazers over T-shirts instead of over collared shirts like normal people. They were chattering about achieving a high score on something called Pac-Man.

"The eighties are weird," Dexter said.

Sarah put her hand on Dexter's shoulder and shook him a little bit, and when she did, he realized that he had been stalling. As exciting as it was to stare at college students from twenty-five years ago and imagine them being his friends' parents, he knew that at some point he had to go back to the present to see if his attempt to force his mother to make better lifestyle choices had succeeded. They had steered Dexter's mom clear of a building that Dexter suspected had asbestos by blocking it off with yellow tape. They secretly signed her up for an aerobics class that advertised its willingness to pound on your door at five a.m., and whose instructor promised that she didn't take no for an answer. They snuck into her dorm room and placed blinders and earplugs on her bed to ensure that she would always get a proper night's sleep.

It was time to face the hospital and all of its assorted medical devices and see if their efforts had worked.

And now that he had seen a new side of his mom, one that he had never even considered existed, it made him want to save her all the more desperately now that he understood there were other parts of her that he had never seen before.

He nodded to Sarah and she handed the time machine over to him. It glinted in the sunlight and almost seemed aware of its own power.

"I'm ready," he said, staring at the key.

Sarah grabbed him on one shoulder and Chloe touched his other.

"I can do this," he said.

He paused for a little while longer before he finally said the words and the air rushed out of his lungs as they warped back to the hospital.

Dexter kept his eyes closed for a moment but knew he

was right back in the hall outside his mother's room. He could smell that strange rubbery hospital smell.

Sarah squeezed his shoulder in solidarity, and then Dexter lost nearly all brain functionality entirely when Chloe pulled him into a tight hug. He was not positive that his feet were still touching the ground, and he was pretty sure his brain had somehow flown straight out of his skull.

"It will be okay," she whispered. "I'm sorry, Dexy."

Chloe broke the hug and Dexter said, "Thank you."

Chloe bit her lip and looked away. Dexter took a deep breath and readied himself to peek inside his mother's hospital room. If they had succeeded, if his mom had stopped smoking and that had somehow cured her of her illness, it would be someone else inside the room.

He crept over. Nodded his head to himself. And peeked inside.

He saw his mom, looking pale and tired, her hair disheveled. She was still there. It hadn't worked.

His shoulders slumped and he turned back to face Sarah and Chloe. Sarah's eyes crinkled in sadness and sympathy, and Dexter straightened his posture and pursed his lips. He wanted to give up. But he couldn't.

"We have to do better," he said.

He was daunted but undeterred. His mom needed him. He knew what she would encourage him to do in this situation. It was the same thing she always told him whenever he felt like giving up: He'd just have to try harder. He could do anything that he put his mind to.

He reached into his pocket. But the time machine wasn't there. His heart skipped a beat. He checked his other pocket and looked around to see if he had dropped it.

"Sorry, Dexy," Chloe said. She had backed away from them and her face was clouded with an expression Dexter couldn't place. Sadness? Sheepishness? Deviousness? Dexter saw the key glinting in one of her small hands.

Dexter couldn't process what he was seeing. "Why do you have that?"

Then he remembered how Chloe had hugged him. She must have stolen it from his pocket while he was distracted.

"You'll understand," Chloe said.

Sarah Daisy ran at her. "You stupid, thieving . . ."

Chloe whispered something to the time machine, shimmered for a brief instant, and warped just before Sarah reached her.

Chapter 25

"**P**ut these in your ears," Mick said.

He pushed two small silver ear buds into Jacob's hands and waited for Jacob to do as he was told. Jacob just stared at them. He had no intention of mixing earwax particles with his arch-nemesis.

"Why should I?" Jacob asked.

Mick rolled back his head and sighed loudly. "Because I have something to show you, but I can't tell you where and when we're going next."

Jacob's face flushed with anger. "Tell me or I'm not going."

Mick closed his eyes and sighed again. He wiped his face and kicked at some leaves.

"It would be too dangerous for you to know. There are people who would do anything for this information." Mick turned back to Jacob, his eyes hard and jaw set. He pointed his finger in Jacob's face. *"Anything."*

Jacob was taken aback. He couldn't recall ever seeing Mick so serious before, not even after Jacob had spray-painted Mick's spaceship. He wondered if it was really possible that people would force Jacob to tell them whatever destination Mick was guarding so closely, and the edge to Mick's voice made Jacob believe that he was telling the truth.

But he still didn't put in the ear buds.

"Tell me the plan," Jacob said.

Mick stared at Jacob and blinked a few times, considering. He took out his time machine. He shook his head slowly. "No. It's too dangerous. Either you put those in and come with me or I'll leave you here in the forest."

It was Jacob's turn to blink.

"Don't think I won't do it," Mick said.

Jacob realized he didn't have much choice. Mick was the one with the time machine.

He put the ear buds in, cringing at the thought that they had once been in Mick's ears. Mick tapped his Astral Telly and Jacob's ears were suddenly blasted with lounge music.

"Ugh!" Jacob shouted. "What is this?"

Mick mouthed words, but Jacob couldn't hear them. "What?" Jacob shouted.

Mick covered his mouth with one hand, grabbed Jacob's shoulder with his other hand, and suddenly the air rushed out of Jacob's lungs and he was warping.

The first thing Jacob noticed when they arrived at their destination was a cold wind that bit at his cheeks. He rubbed his arms for warmth. As his vision adjusted, he also realized it was dark. They had warped into the night.

And when he finally got his bearings, Jacob could hardly believe what he was seeing. He was staring at a very large, very old spaceship.

It was tall and silver, with four fins that touched the ground and curved into a neat point at its very top, which was nearly a hundred feet in the air. The shell of the spaceship looked like rough pounded metal studded with large gray bolts. The only way inside was via a small ladder that led up into the belly of the spaceship. It looked nowhere near as futuristic as the spaceships Praiseworthy or Lucy. It wasn't even as futuristic as the spaceship Swift, the dented old ship that had crash-landed on Numonia. It almost looked as if it had been cobbled out of sheets of aluminum and held together with nothing but some glue and a great deal of hope. It was lit by a large, orange full moon that hung low in the sky, almost as if it were keeping watch over such an unlikely, otherworldly object.

"Where are we?" Jacob asked, realizing they could have warped to another planet that had a similar moon. "Is this Earth?"

Mick looked annoyed that Jacob was still asking questions, before relenting and nodding. "Yeah. We're on Earth."

After he had stared at the spaceship for a while, Jacob began to look at the crowd standing around it. He was startled when Mick clapped him on the back.

"Come on," Mick said. "Let's move closer."

They walked to the edge of the group, which was comprised mainly of middle-aged men and women, but there were some children among them as well. They were all dressed in long knit coats and many were wearing unique hats made of animal fur. Jacob was by no means a fashion expert, but they looked like clothes his great-grandparents wore in old photographs. They clutched old suitcases, which were covered in patterned fabric. Jacob guessed they had warped to somewhere in the middle part of the twentieth century.

Though many people were stomping their feet in the cold, there was also a palpable buzz of excitement. People were smiling, excited, chattering quickly to

each other and laughing. A thin voice managed to rise above the din.

"Excuse me," the voice said, reedy and accented. "Excuse me, friends."

The crowd quieted, and Jacob finally caught a glimpse of where the voice came from. The man's white hair was wild, his eyes were wrinkled and kind. He wore a tweedy bow tie, and he was clutching a wooden megaphone. Jacob was not exactly a history buff, but even he knew who it was: Albert Einstein.

"Thank you," Einstein said when the crowd had quieted. "Thank you, friends. Zis is a momentous occasion and a very exciting one, as I don't have to tell you."

Jacob smiled at his halting politeness. Almost every sentence sounded like Einstein was asking a question, seeing if anyone would contradict his words.

"Zese are exciting times but also ze most difficult we have ever known. Hitler's armies stretch across ze whole of Europe, and we have heard ze tales from loved ones of horrors and suffering. Humankind is close to developing weapons zat are greater zan anything ze world has ever seen. Ze time has come for us to leave zis planet and start a new civilization zat is peaceful and good and based on ze principles of fairness and equality. We will live with ze stars. Zey will give us a better life."

Jacob realized what he was seeing. It was the very beginning of the Astral civilization, when the early Astrals blasted off into space and went thousands of years back in time to start a new civilization that would be ready for Earth when it was technologically advanced enough to be dangerous to them.

These were Mick Cracken's ancestors, on Earth, ready to blast off into space. No. He shook his head, remembering again that he was part Astral. They were his ancestors too. These were the people who spread out among the stars, who went back in time and started a new way of living with spaceships and strange planets and a carefree way of life. These were his great-great-great-great-great-grandparents, standing there in the cold with hopeful smiles, ready to blast off into a universe they had never seen before but trusted would give them a better future.

"We will be Astrals," Einstein said. "Ze stars will be our guides. Space will be our home. And we have packed plenty of corndogs aboard ze ship!"

The crowd cheered. Mick lightly punched Jacob on the shoulder and beckoned him toward a nearby hill. Jacob reluctantly followed, and from a safe distance away, they watched the new Astrals climb the ladder one by one, the kids too, cooperating as they hauled their luggage into the hull and disappeared inside.

Jacob even thought he spotted a man with a crescent head, someone who looked like he might have been Moonman McGillicutty's ancestor.

Soon they tipped over the ladder and closed the hatch, and smoke started emerging from the base of the spaceship. The smoke turned into a mighty roar of fire, and the spaceship shook and shuddered and creaked and then suddenly shot into the sky like a bullet. Jacob felt the heat on his face and craned his neck to watch it soar into space and shrink into a small orange dot, and when he couldn't see it anymore, he turned back to look at the field, which was still singed and smoking from the flames.

The Astrals were on their way to space. And Jacob had seen it.

"Wow," Jacob said, turning to Mick. "Thank you for showing me that."

Jacob expected Mick to reward him with a gloating grin, but instead Mick's expression was grim and serious. He pointed to where the spaceship had blasted off.

"Those are our ancestors. Ours. That is the moment when they blasted off into space to become Astrals."

"Right, so thanks for—"

Mick shook his head. "You're not listening. If someone were to stop that ship from blasting off it would mean no more Astrals and no more space colonies . . .

no *us*. You and me, Jacob. We wouldn't exist. Planet Royale, Planet Archimedes, that dustball of a planet I sent you to . . . None of it."

It dawned on Jacob what Mick meant. If someone wanted to get rid of Astrals, all they had to do was go back in time and stop Father Albert and the first Astrals from going into space. If some evil person stopped those first Astrals, there wouldn't even be such a thing as space humans. No planets, no spaceships . . . No Jacob.

Mick nodded, knowing Jacob understood, and held up his key. "If a time machine fell into the wrong hands, it could mean the end of Astrals as we know it."

Chapter 26

"Steady . . . Steady . . ." Dexter said.

He was crouched at the edge of the forest in front of Sarah's house holding out an orange flower, trying to tempt Nelly into eating it. Nelly's beady eyes were definitely intrigued by the flower. He stayed a safe distance away, darted to the left, stopped and stared for a moment at Sarah and Dexter, then darted to the right.

"We're not going to hurt you," Dexter said quietly.

In a blinding flash, Nelly sprang forward, grabbed the flower in his mouth, ran away toward the stream, leaped across it, and disappeared into the forest before Dexter could even start to pounce.

"What . . ." Dexter said. "That wasn't fair!"

Sarah stared at her Astral Telly. Jacob wasn't answering. Astral Tellys could reach anyone in the universe, but apparently they couldn't find someone stuck in a different time.

She shook her head and stared at the jungle that used to be their street. "What are we going to do, Dexter?"

Dexter sat down on the ground and thought a moment. "Maybe we could set a trap with a box?"

"No," Sarah said. "I mean, what are we going to do now? How are we going to find Jacob? What about your mom? What do we do? We're stuck here without a time machine."

Dexter grabbed another flower and started picking at the petals. "That's a good point."

Sarah sat down behind him and leaned her back against his. Even though she was still mad at Jacob Wonderbar for running off, she was starting to grow worried that he hadn't returned. She felt a pit in her stomach when she thought about the fact that she had no idea whatsoever where or when he was in time. He might even need her to rescue him, but she didn't have a time machine to try and find him.

When she thought about the missing time machine, she felt an electric rush of anger at The Brat for trying

to destroy her life yet again. She was always, always up to no good. Sarah did not know what she had done in a past life to have deserved growing up with the worst kid sister the universe had ever known, but it must have been extremely severe. There were not enough words in the dictionary for Sarah to describe the depth of the anger she felt. The Brat had even deprived her supposed crush Dexter of a chance to fix things with his mom.

However frustrated she may have been with Jacob, she was completely consumed with anger for her sister. What did she even need the time machine for? What did she think she was doing? It didn't make any sense.

"So . . ." Dexter said. "What should we do? Do you think I could eat dinner at your house?"

"Of course," Sarah said. "But first we should—"

Sarah heard a rustling in the forest down the street. She craned her neck. She realized it was a person. A girl, she corrected. She thought it was her sister and she was ready to pounce, but then her heart sank.

Former princess and current vice president of the universe, Catalina Penelope Cassandra Crackenarium, the twelve-year-old version, walked out of the forest and squealed when she saw Sarah and Dexter. "There you are!"

She ran over and stood in front of them and jumped up and down a few times.

Sarah didn't get up. She thought she might be sick. "Of course it's you," she managed to say.

"What did I miss?" Catalina asked, clapping her hands.

Jacob and Mick stood in the dim light. The last embers from the rocket had been extinguished and the orange moon cast a faint glow onto the hill and surrounding field. The wind picked up and Jacob shivered against the cold.

"Who are they?" Jacob asked.

Mick gave Jacob a grave stare and Jacob shivered again, unsure whether he was reacting to the wind or the seriousness of Mick's demeanor. Jacob thought back to their time in Napoleon's France: Dexter's stories about the strange secret society, the old book he found about exterminating space humans, the anxious shouts and gunfire outside the basement, and the angry, twisted face he saw through the doorway before they warped to safety.

"What are we up against?" Jacob asked.

The idea of strange and dangerous anti-Astrals made him nervous, but he had to know what they were facing. If Mick was right, there were people out there who hated Astrals so much, they didn't even want Jacob to exist in the first place.

Mick slowly raised his hand, clutching the time machine. "Tower of London, Earth, November fourth, 1525, four p.m.," he said quietly. He stared at Jacob. "Are you ready?"

Jacob grabbed on to the key.

"Warp," Mick said.

The air rushed out of Jacob's lungs and when he opened his eyes he found himself staring at an imposing white stone building that rose up above a carefully manicured green lawn. Two black ravens eyed Jacob and Mick and squawked angrily at them. They were in a courtyard surrounded by tall stone walls and dotted with white wooden buildings with red roofs. The sun hung low in the sky, casting long shadows. It was eerily quiet, and Jacob wondered if the castle was deserted.

Mick seemed to be having the same thoughts. He darted his eyes around every corner of the castle, then beckoned Jacob to follow him. Mick crouched as he ran over to one of the courtyard walls, looking back

over his shoulder from time to time as if he could be struck by a stray arrow or spear at any moment. Jacob mimicked him and ran to the wall as fast as he could. He did not much feel like getting impaled by brutish medieval soldiers.

Mick took one last look around and then ducked through a small wooden door. Jacob followed him. They were in a dark passage underneath the walls. The air was dank and smelled like mildew. Mick took out his Astral Telly, which he held in front of him for light. Jacob heard a small scratching sound and barely stopped himself from shouting out when a large rat ran past his feet. Mick slammed himself against the wall and held his throat in panic, his eyes as wide as saucers.

Jacob smiled at Mick's reaction and said, "What, you're scared of—"

"Shh," Mick whispered angrily, grabbing Jacob's shirt. Jacob kept his mouth shut but kept smiling.

They kept walking and eventually reached a door. Mick paused for a moment, then opened it quickly and they stepped inside a small room lit by just a few candles and a fireplace. A narrow slit in the wall overlooked the moat of the Tower of London and also happened to allow the horrendous smell of the moat to fill the room with a stench of rotting garbage and raw sewage.

"I've been expecting you," a voice said from a desk.

A pale kid with matted yellow hair sat at a desk overflowing with maps and papers and . . . models of planets. Jacob looked around the room again. It looked like a typical small wood-paneled medieval room that wouldn't have seemed out of place in a museum, only the walls were covered with paintings of planets and stars and diagrams of spaceships and things that strange medieval teenagers were not supposed to have known about.

He wore a plain brown robe and a gold triangle around his neck. His eyes were coal black and fiery.

"This is Luger Smythe," Mick said, his voice clipped and precise. "Founder of the Strangers."

Luger smiled, revealing broken yellow teeth. "Is that what you *aliens* call us? I might have known."

Mick bristled at Luger's use of the A-word, the gravest insult someone could call an Astral. But even though Jacob suspected he could have broken Luger Smythe in half just by breathing on him the wrong way, Mick didn't attack him. Instead he stood as rigid as a statue with his fists clenched.

Some of Luger's papers fluttered in a foul breeze that swept in from the slit in the castle wall. Even though Luger was living in a smelly room in the Tower of London, Jacob had a feeling that Luger was

an extremely important person. Very few people in medieval England probably got to live in the castle unless they were about to have their heads chopped off, and Luger clearly was not a prisoner. Jacob wondered if he was the author of *On the Origin and Danger of Human Species Not Originating on Our Planet,* the anti-Astral tome he had seen in Napoleon's palace in France in 1804.

Luger smiled, which had the opposite effect of most smiles. Rather than radiating happiness, his smile sent a shadow around the room. "His Majesty King Henry the Eighth brought me to the Tower because he understands the threat that the space menace represents. The space menace will destroy us all. I have foreseen it." His voice was reedy and high-pitched, with a strange English accent.

"How do you know we're from space?" Jacob asked.

"Your pantaloons," Luger spat.

Jacob looked down and realized he was wearing jeans. "Oh, good point." He thought about telling Luger that the jeans were invented on Earth and that they were from the future, but he figured the distinction would be lost on Luger. Besides, he really was half Astral.

"Why do you hate us?" Jacob asked.

Luger looked Jacob over as if he were sizing him

up. "Aliens have brought trouble to Earth from the beginning of time. They have no shame. They want to destroy us all. Just as they destroyed my family's home and livestock when they dropped a giant snowball on it."

Jacob managed to stifle a laugh when he pictured an Astral spaceship hauling a huge snowball. He cleared his throat and grimaced instead. "That sounds terrible," he said.

"I came to see you," Mick said. "To see if you would change your mind about us. We're two Astrals and we're here in peace."

Luger smiled even wider and Jacob thought he noticed the candles dimming as a result. "I know who you are," he said to Mick.

Mick raised his eyebrows in surprise. "You . . . you do?"

"Yes." Luger pointed a bony finger at Mick. "You're the last leader Astrals will ever know."

Chapter 28

W hat are you doing here?" Sarah asked Catalina.

Catalina bounced up and down and then hugged Sarah.

"Ugh," Sarah said.

Catalina broke the hug and said, "Well. My silly brother warped away and I got really bored, so I thought I would take a trip to see my best friends in the universe. Dexy! You look so mature!"

"Um. Thanks," Dexter said.

"Where's Jakey?" Catalina asked.

Sarah gritted her teeth. "*Jakey* warped away with your brother and we don't know where they are. And my stupid sister stole our time machine."

"Oh," Catalina said, looking crestfallen. "I guess you'll have to do."

Sarah pressed her lips together at more of Catalina's rudeness, but then her eyes widened when she had an idea. "Do you have a time machine?!"

"Of course not!" Catalina said. "Mick took off with ours. I had the scientists send me here with the 'Vault' time machine that we used to send you guys back to Earth way back when."

Sarah felt a rush of blood to her head. Not only did she find Catalina terrifically annoying, she didn't even bring anything helpful to Earth. Not a spaceship, not a time machine. They were stuck with her.

Sarah had made peace with the princess-turned-vice-president after they had joined forces in a last-ditch and unsuccessful effort to help Jacob win the presidential election, but Sarah was growing too worried about Jacob to feel calm enough to deal with Catalina. She didn't trust that if Jacob were to return, he wouldn't go gaga over Catalina like he usually did, and Sarah had a mind to . . .

"Sarah?" Dexter asked.

"What?!" Sarah turned on him with her hands on her hips.

"I'm really hungry," he said.

Sarah exhaled and let her hands drop. "Sorry, Dex." She stared at the ground for a moment. She was hungry too. Food first, then they could decide what to do. "I guess we can go eat in my house."

"Yay!" Catalina said. "Can I see your room? Can I try on your clothes? Oh. Never mind. I forgot who I was talking to. Fashion nightmare."

Sarah started walking toward her door without a word, thinking Catalina and Dexter would trail behind, but she had to wait when Dexter started telling Catalina about his mom. Sarah softened a little toward Catalina when she heard how genuinely sympathetic Catalina sounded. She asked a million questions and hugged Dexter and she could tell from the sound of Dexter's voice that she had succeeded in making him feel just a bit better.

Sarah stopped them when they reached her door. Dexter looked terrified and Catalina looked extremely excited.

"Just . . ." Sarah started to say.

"Yes?" Catalina asked happily.

Sarah sighed. "Please don't embarrass me."

"I won't," Dexter said quickly.

"Not you," Sarah said, giving Catalina a cold look.

"Oh, silly," Catalina said. "I'm so happy I get to meet your family!"

Sarah grunted and threw open the door. "Mom?" she called out.

They walked through the house into the kitchen, where her mom was sipping a cup of coffee. "Hi, darling," her mom said. "I . . ."

Sarah's mom gave a start when she saw Catalina and Dexter and she almost spilled her coffee.

"Catal . . ." Sarah's mom started to say, but stopped herself.

Sarah's jaw dropped in shock. "You know her?!"

Sarah's mom composed herself, and the momentary look of surprise was gone so quickly, Sarah almost wondered if she had imagined it. Her mom gave a friendly smile to Catalina and Dexter. "Sure honey, isn't this one of your friends from school?"

"No," Sarah said carefully.

"You must be hungry," Sarah's mom said. "Do you guys want a snack?"

"Yeah, can we have some corndogs?" Sarah asked.

Sarah's mom was aghast. "Corndogs! In the name of Phil, why would you ask your mother for something cooked in oil?" She shuddered. "You can have arugula salad and cucumber quinoa like normal children."

"Oh," Dexter said, trying to cover his disappointment. "Yay, Phil."

Sarah's mom brought out the food and they devoured it even though it was not the corn-battered deliciousness they had hoped for. Sarah watched her mom out of the corner of her eye and noticed that her mom was watching Catalina out of the corner of *her* eye. She almost looked excited to see her.

Did they really know each other? Could her mom have known that Catalina was the former princess of the universe?

"Where's Jacob?" Sarah's mom asked. She tried to sound casual, but Sarah heard an edge in her voice.

"Um. Not here?" Sarah said.

"Don't get smart with me, young lady," Sarah's mom said. Sarah averted her eyes from her mom's fierce gaze. She hated when her mom yelled at her in front of her friends. She felt like running away, but she knew that would only make it worse.

"I think it's high time that you moved along from that troublemaker. You need more friends like Dexter, who are positive influences in your life."

"Um. Thank you?" Dexter said. If Mrs. Daisy noticed that Dexter appeared older, she didn't mention it.

Sarah's mom tapped the table with her finger with finality. "I don't want to see you spending any more time with Jacob Wonderbar. None. Period. End of story."

"Mom!" Sarah shrieked.

"You heard me," her mom said. "And if I hear about you fraternizing with him at school, you will be grounded for a month."

Sarah seethed with anger. She might have thought that Jacob was a jerk to have ditched her, but he was still her friend. She didn't know why her mom couldn't see Jacob like she saw him. Her parents were always trying to stop her from spending any time with Jacob and ruling her life. Sure, he got into trouble and wasn't

the best at school, but he was really smart no matter what his grades may have been, and it wasn't fair that her parents tried to stop them from being friends.

He was fun and he was her best friend and there was nothing her mom could do about that.

"Mrs. Daisy, if I may . . ." Catalina said.

Sarah's mom cleared her throat and pointed toward the front door. "Young lady, I think it's time you went straight on home."

Chapter 29

How did he know you were the president of the universe? He was just some weird kid living in a castle."

Jacob was lounging in the sand on an incredibly beautiful beach in Hawaii in the 1600s. It was lined with lush green trees and the weather was perfectly sunny and warm. Jacob had suggested that he and Mick take a break in a safe place to regroup and come up with a plan. He had also realized that the time machine made for a rather fantastic vacation device.

"Well, Wonderbar," Mick said in a highly condescending tone, "there are two possibilities. Either he can see the future or he got his hands on a time machine." Mick lay flat on the sand with his arms outstretched. "Do you believe in psychic powers?"

Jacob watched some natives out in the water surfing with long wooden boards. They waved at Jacob and Mick and didn't seem to find it odd that two mysterious people were relaxing on their beach.

"No," Jacob said. "I don't believe in psychic powers."

Jacob began to recognize the seriousness of Luger recognizing Mick. If Luger knew who Mick was, he probably had a time machine. If he had a time machine, he and the other Strangers could band together and stop the original Astrals from blasting off into space.

If that were true, Mick really could be the last Astral leader. They were in grave danger.

"But we're still here," Jacob said, staring at his hands to reassure himself. "If the Strangers had already succeeded, we wouldn't exist, right? No Astrals, no us?"

Mick closed his eyes against the sun and reluctantly nodded. Jacob felt temporarily better, but the idea of suddenly disappearing as if he had never existed in the first place gave him chills. He wouldn't even know the Strangers had won. He would just be gone.

"So let's go back in time and stop Luger," Jacob said. "We know he started the Strangers, why don't we stop him from doing that and then we'll be safe? Maybe we can burn up all his papers so he can't write that book."

Mick nodded. "You're finally getting it."

"Why do they hate Astrals?" Jacob asked. "I mean, yeah, Luger had a snowball dropped on his house, but what about the rest of them? I don't get it."

Mick rose up on an elbow and gave Jacob a cold look. "You're part Earther, why don't you tell me?"

Jacob blinked and thought about Patrick Gravy and the SEERs, the Astrals who had such wrong ideas about Earth that they wanted to blow it up entirely. They were just as scary as the Strangers, but what made them so crazy?

They were scared, Jacob realized. It was easy to think they were brave because they had big guns and strutted around like they were the toughest guys in the universe, but deep down they were more scared of Earth than anyone else.

There may have been some truth to the fact that Astrals represented a threat to Earth, but Luger Smythe and the Strangers had taken that bit of truth too far. They let their fear turn into hate.

"So what should we do?" Jacob asked.

Mick sat up and brushed sand off his arms. "Now we stop them."

Jacob looked out at the ocean and saw a whale rise up out of the water and splash down. He considered

Mick's suggestion. Jacob recognized the threat that Earth represented to the Astral civilization, but he wasn't sure what they should do to prevent it.

Jacob didn't know how to stop the Strangers, but Mick seemed to have an idea.

"It's time to plan a prank on Luger Smythe," Mick said.

Chapter 30

Sarah sprawled on the ground in the clearing in the forest downstream from their houses as Dexter and Catalina tried unsuccessfully to cheer her up.

She didn't know why her mom was so mean. She was always forcing Sarah to do more and more extra-curriculars and study harder and she never ever stopped to tell Sarah she was doing a good job. Just a few weeks ago Sarah had gotten a perfect 100 on her pre-algebra test and when she showed her mom her score, she just nodded as if that was what was expected, not even a success worth celebrating. And now she was trying to stop Sarah from seeing her best friend in the universe.

It wasn't fair. She was barely able to see Jacob outside of school already, and now her mom wanted to take what little time she had left away from her.

Worse, Sarah didn't even know if Jacob was safe.

"Is she going to be okay?" Dexter asked.

"I don't know," Catalina said. "She seems pretty upset."

"I'm right here!" Sarah shouted. She appreciated their concern, but she couldn't calm herself down. Her mom had embarrassed her in front of Catalina and Dexter, after she had been worried that it would be Catalina who would make a mess out of things. It made her feel even worse that she was the one crying, when she remembered that Dexter had something much more serious to worry about. She felt weak, and that was the worst feeling Sarah knew.

Catalina took out her Telly and dialed. She handed it to Sarah, who took it before she could wonder who Catalina was calling. Sarah's mind was whisked to the spaceship Praiseworthy.

"Mistress Daisy!" Praiseworthy shouted. "Galloping grasshoppers, this is a wonderful surprise!"

Praiseworthy was painted orange and the dainty horse sculptures on his hull were ornamented with streamers. Sarah sniffed and walked on board and plopped herself into the captain's chair, kicking up her feet on the console. She didn't have to worry about breaking anything because she wasn't really there.

"Hi Praiseworthy," she said.

"Whatever is the matter?"

"I don't know what to do," Sarah said. "My mom is so mean and I don't know where to find Jacob."

"Oh, dearest me," Praiseworthy said. "Mistress Daisy, I am ever so sorry. I don't have parents other than some large sheets of plastic and metal, but I don't see how anyone could possibly be mean to you."

"Thanks," Sarah sighed. Praiseworthy was always able to say the right things.

Sarah took some deep breaths. Her nose was stuffed up and she still felt very shaky.

"What should I do?" she asked.

"Mistress Daisy, if there is anything I have learned about you, it is that you are one of the smartest human beings I have had the pleasure of knowing. If you follow your heart, I am quite confident you will find whatever it is you are looking for."

Sarah nodded. She knew he was right. She was worried and scared, but there wasn't anything she could do about her mom at the moment. All she could do was to be patient and wait and when the right opportunity presented itself, she would follow her heart.

"I will. Thank you, Praiseworthy." She wanted

to hug him, but it was rather difficult to hug a large spaceship. "You're the best spaceship in the universe."

"Oh dearest me, coming from you, I cannot imagine a greater compliment. I am overjoyed!"

"Bye, Praiseworthy. Take care."

Sarah ended the call and she was back in the forest. She handed the Telly over to Catalina, who looked on anxiously. Sarah would never have thought to call Praiseworthy to cheer herself up, but somehow Catalina had known exactly what she needed. The princess always found a way to make it back into Sarah's good graces no matter how rude she was most of the time.

"Thanks." Sarah sniffed.

"That's what friends are for!" Catalina said happily.

Sarah still wasn't sure that they were friends, but she didn't contradict Catalina. Maybe they were after all.

There was a rustling in the forest, and when Sarah turned to see who was approaching, she flushed with anger all over again.

The Brat was back.

Chapter 31

T his isn't going to work," Jacob said.

Mick sized up the young elephant, which looked back at him with kind, watery eyes. Although he was small for an elephant, he was still huge and was significantly taller than Jacob and Mick. He had rough gray skin and was covered in a red cape. He reached out his trunk and flipped Mick's hair.

"Yep," Mick said. "I think it will."

They were at the London zoo in 1865, which, as Jacob suspected, had rather shoddy security. Mick had warped them straight inside the zoo, and since the only guard was a sleepy constable who sat outside the main entrance, they didn't have to worry about getting into trouble.

As they wandered around the zoo in the moonlight,

Jacob was shocked at the appalling conditions of the animals. They lived in tiny cages and did not appear to be very well taken care of. Many of them screeched at Jacob and rattled their cages as he walked by. When he and Mick were finished with their prank, Jacob figured he would need to send some animal rights activists back in time to improve the living conditions of old zoos.

After a short while they found the elephant they were looking for. According to a sign at the front of his cage, the elephant's name was Jumbo and he was four years old. He also apparently had a personality problem, as there were many danger signs to that effect around his cage, but he seemed friendly enough to Jacob.

"I think I know about this elephant," Jacob said, distantly recalling a story his mom read him when he was little. "This is where the word *jumbo* comes from. Because of this one elephant. He was really popular."

Mick shrugged. He held up the time machine and waved it between two fingers. "Ready?"

Jacob didn't answer and stared for a moment at the time machine, which was well within his grasp. Mick now trusted him enough that it didn't cross his mind that Jacob would try to take it.

If there was ever an opportunity for Jacob to steal it and maroon Mick, this was it. He didn't believe in

Mick's plan. He didn't think Luger Smythe was going to change his mind about Astrals just because of an elephant prank. Mick had let his guard down.

But he decided he would give Mick a chance. Jacob looked Mick in the eye and reached out and grabbed on to the key. "All right. Let's do this."

Mick warped the two of them straight back into Luger Smythe's room in the Tower of London.

"You again," Luger spat when he saw them appear. "You have overstayed your welcome, aliens. Get out of here before I have you both impaled on the end of a spear."

Jacob wasn't sure how someone so evil could also seem so harmless. He didn't think Luger would really call the guards on them, and he couldn't even look Mick and Jacob in the eye. Jacob suspected that hating people was a lot easier when you could just pretend that they're horrible monsters. Though he worried this prank was about to confirm it.

Mick smiled. "I don't think you like us very much."

Luger sneered back at him. "I would like you to never exist at all."

"But isn't there something we haven't really talked about?" Mick asked.

Luger clutched his blanket tighter around his neck. "And what might that be?"

"The elephant in the room," Mick said.

Luger blinked. "The what?"

"You know, the elephant in the room."

"I'm sure I haven't the slightest idea what you're saying," Luger said.

Jacob and Mick warped back to the zoo and grabbed on to Jumbo's trunk. Jacob nodded, Mick nodded, and Jacob crossed his fingers that warping with a four-year-old elephant wouldn't break the space-time continuum.

When he opened his eyes back in the Tower of London, Luger was pressed against the arrow slit, terrified. Jacob and Mick were pressed against the wall. And Jumbo, who took up nearly every bit of available space, did not seem particularly alarmed to have found himself in a strange room in a medieval castle. He plucked an apple off of Luger's desk and threw it into his mouth. Then he ran his trunk across Luger's desk, sending the papers flying into the air.

"Sorcery!" Luger screeched. "Evil sorcery! Get this beast out of here!"

There was absolutely no way Jumbo would be able to fit through the door. Jumbo picked up a model of a planet and rolled it around on the ground before stepping on it and smashing it to pieces.

"You beast!" Luger shouted. "Do not do that!"

Jumbo ruffled Luger's hair. Luger shrieked.

Jacob and Mick ran out the door and stood just outside it.

"Don't . . . don't leave me here with this thing!" Luger shouted.

"Surrender!" Mick yelled.

Jacob took a deep breath and hoped Luger could be persuaded. "If we get rid of the elephant," Jacob said reasonably, "will you give up your fight against the Astrals?"

"Never," Luger said. Jacob's heart began to sink.

Luger batted Jumbo with a book, but Jumbo seemed to think it was a fun game and batted Luger right back.

"I'm sorry about your house, but Astrals don't mean you any harm," Jacob said. "If you just let it go, we'll get rid of the elephant."

"I will never surrender to the space menace," Luger said.

Jacob shook his head. Of course the plan wasn't working. The survival of Astrals was on the line and all Mick could think to do was play a prank.

Although Jacob did have to admit the expression on Luger's face was rather amusing.

"Say uncle," Mick said to Luger.

"Uncle?" Luger asked, confused. "Why would I say that word?"

Jacob and Mick looked at each other and shrugged. Apparently that phrase hadn't been invented yet.

"Let's get out of here," Jacob said.

Mick walked back in, intentionally scattered some more of Luger's papers, and grabbed on to Jumbo.

Mick smiled. "What time is it when an elephant sits on your desk?"

Luger stared at Mick, refusing to rise to the bait.

"Time for a new desk," Mick said.

Jacob laughed despite himself, but he saw Luger edge over to his desk and open a drawer.

"Mick . . ." Jacob said.

Luger pulled out a key.

"Mick!" Jacob yelled.

Mick warped them back to the zoo with Jumbo, who seemed relieved to see his cage and stepped right in.

Mick high-fived Jacob and tried to give him a chest bump, but Jacob just stepped aside. Their plan hadn't worked, and Jacob couldn't understand why Mick had ever thought it would. Someone like Luger Smythe wouldn't be deterred by blackmail, no matter how big an elephant was trapped in his study. If anything, it would strengthen his resolve.

And although Jacob hadn't gotten a good look at the key, it appeared that Luger already had a time machine. They were in grave danger.

The survival of Astrals was at stake and Jacob strongly suspected Mick hadn't the slightest idea what he was doing.

Chapter 32

W hat did you do?!" Sarah shouted at Chloe.

Chloe crossed her arms and gave her sister a smug grin. "Why should I tell you?"

It took every ounce of self-control Sarah possessed to stop herself from pouncing on her little sister. It was bad enough that she had stolen the time machine from Dexter when he was already worried about his mother. Now she was standing there looking like nothing at all was wrong. She should have been apologizing and begging their forgiveness, not gloating. Sarah didn't want to give Chloe the satisfaction of reacting to her bait, but Chloe was an expert at pushing her buttons.

"Dexter?" Sarah muttered. "Can you please ask my worm of a sister what she was doing stealing our time machine?"

"Oh, okay," Dexter said. He turned to Chloe. "What were you doing with our time machine, Chloe?"

Chloe batted her eyelashes at Dexter for a moment before she noticed Catalina.

"Who are you?" Chloe asked with a tremor in her voice.

Catalina didn't betray any hint of noticing Chloe's hesitation. "You must be Sarah Daisy's better-looking sister!" she exclaimed.

Sarah's ears burned. It was becoming an extremely difficult day.

Catalina extended her hand. "I'm Catalina Cassandra Penelope Crackenarium, it's so nice to meet you."

Chloe sneered at Catalina's hand and grunted. "I'm sure."

Catalina put her hand down in confusion and Dexter stepped over toward Chloe, keeping an eye on Sarah as he moved closer. "Hi. Um, Chloe? So, what were you doing with the time machine? If you don't mind me asking?"

Chloe's doe eyes returned and she smiled sweetly at Dexter. "Helping you, of course."

Sarah scoffed. "Sure. Tell us what you were really doing."

Chloe turned on Sarah and met her fiery gaze. "I was! I went into the future to see what would happen

with Dexy's mom." She took his hand and patted it gently. "So he wouldn't have to worry."

"What . . ." Dexter whispered. "What did you . . ."

"She's going to be fine!" Chloe said. "It's no big deal. She gets out of the hospital in a few days, it's not life-threatening at all. It didn't even have anything to do with smoking, she just had a skin thing."

Dexter sighed in relief and held his face in his hands. "Thanks, Chlo. Thank you so much."

Sarah stared at her sister. "I don't believe you."

Chloe took the time machine out of her pocket and waved it at Sarah. "Bet you a million dollars. Take the time machine right now and go see for yourself. You never believe me about anything. Why don't you go see how smart you are?"

Sarah didn't reach for the time machine and instead kept staring at Chloe. She sensed that Chloe wasn't actually bluffing, and she believed that if she did go into the future, she would see that Dexter's mom really was safe. Sarah's heart softened a bit. It was nice that Chloe was brave enough to go see what would happen so that Dexter didn't have to worry.

But something still wasn't adding up.

"But Chloe, if that's all you wanted to do, why wouldn't you just tell us?" Sarah asked. "Why did you have to go and steal the time machine?"

Chloe gave Sarah an evil grin. "Because now I can do this."

Chloe whispered into the time machine, yelled "Warp!" and disappeared before Sarah could reach for it.

She was going to kill her sister if she could ever catch her again.

"She's gone," Dexter said. He sounded quite lost.

There was yet another rustling in the forest, and Sarah charged toward it, thinking Chloe had warped back again to trick them.

But instead she found herself face-to-face with the middle-aged Mick Cracken. His shoulders were slumped and he looked terrifically sad. His shirt was ripped and he was clutching a half-eaten box of donuts.

Old Mick sighed loudly. "I want to go home now."

Chapter 33

Back to business," Mick said.

Mick and Jacob were having a regrouping session on the top of a mountain on Planet Stupendia, known for its incredible natural wonders. Jacob remembered the planet from the time when Sarah Daisy had staged a campaign rally and he had spray-painted graffiti on Mick's spaceship. Green forests and turquoise lakes and golden valleys spread out before them, and Jacob tried to ignore the sheer thousand-foot drops that fell precipitously from their perch atop the mountain. Although they were high up in the sky, the air was pleasant and warm with only a soft breeze disturbing the calm.

Mick took a yellow piece of folded parchment out

of his pocket and handed it to Jacob. "I spotted this in Luger's room."

Jacob unfolded the paper and his heart skipped a beat. It was an ink drawing of Chloe Daisy. An ink drawing from hundreds of years before Chloe Daisy was even born.

"This is impossible!" Jacob said.

Mick stared impassively at Jacob, as if he was waiting for him to figure out what he was seeing.

Jacob stared again at the paper. There was no mistake. It was definitely Chloe Daisy, The Brat, the ruiner of good times and one of the most annoying individuals Jacob had ever met in his life.

Jacob wasn't as slow as Mick thought he was. There was only one explanation. "Chloe must have gotten her hands on a time machine," Jacob said.

Jacob had no idea how Chloe even knew who Luger Smythe was, but the only way she could have possibly appeared on a drawing from the 1500s was if she had warped back to the past or if Luger had somehow warped to the future. It also explained why Luger had known who Mick was. She must have gone farther back in time than Jacob and Mick had, and given it to him then.

Mick gave Jacob an exaggerated and patronizing

pat on the back, as if Jacob were a dull pupil who had finally learned to spell *cat*. But Jacob had realized more than that.

"And there's absolutely no reason you should know who Chloe is."

Mick stopped patting Jacob and sucked in his breath.

Jacob knew he had caught Mick off guard, but he didn't take much pleasure from it. Instead he was deeply disappointed.

He had just been thinking he and Mick were on a team. That maybe Mick had changed or that he was wrong about him. That maybe, just maybe, Mick had a conscience and could be counted on in a dangerous pinch. But now he had caught him holding out on him again.

Mick had slipped up. He had never met Chloe, at least not in front of Jacob. Mick hadn't been there when they went back to see dinosaurs, and Chloe hadn't been there in the Palais des Tuileries when Mick had arrived out of nowhere. Jacob had no idea how Mick knew Chloe existed, but he did know Mick was still playing his own game, with his own motives and own secrets. He was only telling Jacob as much as he needed to keep Jacob doing what he wanted him to do.

And Jacob realized that he had gotten so caught up

in the Strangers and Luger Smythe that he had lost track of what he should have been doing: finding his dad. Jacob trusted his mom more than anyone in the world, and she had told him he had to find his father. That was what he needed to do.

"Look," Mick said carefully. "Maybe I know more about what's happening than I've let on. It's not diabolical that I know who Sarah's sister is; I did some research during my planning so I would be ready for everything. But you're right. I haven't told you everything. You have to trust me that I have my reasons."

"Out with it, then," Jacob said. "Tell me everything."

Mick stood up and stepped to the edge of the cliff. He shuffled his toes to the edge and looked down at the abyss. He turned back to face Jacob. He smiled and said, "You just have to trust me."

Then Mick leaned back and tumbled off the cliff. Into the abyss. Jacob rushed to the edge and stared down in a panic. He couldn't see Mick at all. Then he heard Mick laughing behind him.

He turned around and saw Mick doubled over laughing, clutching the time machine. He had warped back to safety.

"You should have seen the look on your face!" Mick said, barely able to get the words out. "You were so

worried! Wonderbar, I didn't know you cared."

Jacob didn't think it was funny. "Take me back to the present," he said through clenched teeth.

He needed to get back to his friends. Sarah would know what to do. And if Chloe had a time machine, it meant that she had somehow gotten ahold of Sarah's. Sarah could be in danger, and Jacob needed to join forces with her.

Mick held out the time machine. "Definitely, Wonderbar. I'll take you back to the present."

Mick smiled wide. "You can trust me."

Jacob glared at Mick. He knew that wasn't true. But he grabbed on to the time machine and they warped.

Chapter 34

No one moved at first when Jacob and Mick warped back into the clearing. Sarah looked happy to see Jacob, but sensed that something was wrong. Old Mick dropped his box of donuts. Dexter looked very confused.

Catalina broke the silence. "Jakey!" she shouted as she ran over to envelop him in a hug. "I've been looking all over for you! We need to talk."

"Wow, hi," Jacob said. "When did you get here?"

But he broke the hug quickly and rushed over to hug Sarah. She buried her face in his shoulder and said, "I'm glad you're okay, but you're a jerk for leaving me behind."

"I know," he said. "I'm sorry."

He nodded and bumped fists with Dexter, shook

his head with dismay at Old Mick, then turned his attention back to Young Mick. Jacob pointed at him warily.

"I don't trust this guy," he said.

Sarah cackled. "You don't say . . ."

"But listen," Jacob said. "I learned a lot about what's going on. Those bizarre anti-Astral people are called the Strangers. They want to completely stop Astrals from even existing. If they succeed, I would just disappear, like I never lived in the first place. And here's the worst part: Chloe is mixed up with them somehow."

He handed the parchment drawing to Sarah. "Mick found this in the 1500s, with this creepy kid called Luger Smythe. He started the Strangers."

"Why, Chloe, why?" Sarah sighed. "Jake, she got hold of our time machine."

"I figured," Jacob said. He rested his hand on her shoulder. "How does Chloe know about the Strangers?"

Sarah shook her head. "I don't know."

Jacob felt responsible for Chloe ending up with the time machine. He should have stayed focused on his plan. He should have convinced Mick to warp straight to the present. He should have listened to his mom. But now they could start setting things right.

"We need to find my dad," Jacob said.

"No!" Mick shouted with such force that even Old Mick jumped in surprise. "We have to stop the Strangers. I have a plan."

"I want to go home," Old Mick said.

"Not yet!" Young Mick said.

"You're not the boss of me," Old Mick said, stepping over to Young Mick and putting his hands on his hips. "I'm bigger than you are."

"Maybe that's because you need to go on a diet," Young Mick said.

"Maybe you need to have a better attitude," Old Mick said.

"Um. You're the same person," Dexter said.

Old Mick shook his head. "No way. I'm older. Smarter. Wiser."

"Let's not fight, darlings," Catalina said.

For a moment everyone stood still in the clearing. There was a slight rustle and Nelly came running past in a green blur, barely pausing when he saw the children, and kept right on running. Dexter smacked his head.

Then, one by one, everyone turned their attention to Young Mick, possessor of the sole time machine, the one thing that could change everything.

There was an ominous pause. And all at once they attacked him.

"Get him!" Old Mick said.

"No! No!" Young Mick shouted.

They all grappled for the time machine. Mick held on tightly. He grunted as Old Mick stepped on his foot and Sarah pulled on his ear and Jacob tried to twist his wrist.

Then Old Mick shouted, "Planet Cocoa Chocolate Factory, August eighth, 1872, warp!"

Jacob, Sarah, Dexter, Catalina, Young Mick, and Old Mick were warped directly into a factory with an overpowering and thoroughly delectable aroma of pure chocolate. It looked more like a laboratory than a food-processing center, with teams of Astrals hovering

over small pieces of chocolates and meticulously tending to them as if they were fine jewels.

"Oh my stars, 1872," Old Mick sighed. "My favorite vintage."

Old Mick let go of the time machine and ran over to stuff his face with chocolate. The children didn't let up, however, and kept on grappling for the time machine.

"Mick Jr., May sixteenth, 2012, six p.m., warp!" Mick shouted.

They were warped onto Mick's dimly lit spaceship, full of Mick Cracken–signed graffiti art. Soft lounge music was playing and Jacob could almost feel the

Mick Cracken-ness of the place oozing through his skin.

"Mick Jr.!" Mick shouted. "Freeze them out. Hit them with the targeted temperature settings."

"With pleasure," Mick Jr. said.

Jacob felt a blast of cold air that chilled him to the bone. He was pretty sure his hair was starting to freeze into icicles. He wouldn't be able to hold on long.

"My wedding day, warp!" Catalina shouted.

Jacob closed his eyes when he heard those words. He had a momentary flash of panic that maybe someday Catalina would have succeeded in convincing him to marry her and he would see himself standing dumbly at the front of a procession waiting for Catalina to come down the aisle. But he forced himself to open his eyes and instead just saw an older Catalina sitting in front of a mirror. She looked beautiful and happy and was wearing a white dress studded with brilliant lights.

"Look at my dress!" Catalina shrieked. "Gorgeous!"

Older Catalina turned around and winked. "Hi, darling," she said. "Stay fabulous."

"I will," Catalina whispered.

The children kept grappling with the time machine and no one was willing to let go. Jacob knew exactly where he wanted to warp.

"My house, April fifth, 2010, warp!" Jacob shouted.

"That's . . ." Dexter said before the air was sucked out of his lungs.

They came to in front of Jacob's house, and Jacob used all his might to pull the group behind a bush. The street was still a jungle, but other than the ivy growing up the walls of Jacob's house, the front yard still looked the same.

"What are we doing here?" Mick asked.

Sarah flicked her eyes at Jacob before giving Mick a stern stare that warned him not to push it. "It's Jake's birthday," she said.

Jacob signaled for everyone to be quiet, and even though no one let go of the time machine, everyone stopped struggling for control and watched to see what would happen. The door burst open and Jacob saw his dad emerge with a younger version of himself trailing behind. Young Jacob had a huge smile on his face and he was skipping around, so excited to see what was going to happen.

It was Jacob's last birthday before his dad moved away from home, and he remembered every moment. Jacob's dad had always made his birthdays special, but this one had been especially spectacular.

Jacob's heart raced when he watched his dad. It was the first time he had seen him in years, and his

175

memory hadn't faded a bit. He had messy hair and a slightly receding hairline, wore a buttoned shirt with a wrinkled collar, and his feet were always moving.

Young Jacob was clutching a map that had been drawn on an old piece of paper. His dad had told him that he had discovered a long-lost pirate map, and only Jacob could find where the treasure was buried. Jacob suspected that his dad had drawn the map, but when he marked off seven paces from the mulberry tree out in front, he stared down at fresh green grass. If his dad had decided shortly before Jacob's birthday to hide something there, how could he have gotten the grass to grow back? Jacob never remembered a hole in that spot in the entire time they lived there.

"I can dig up the lawn?" Young Jacob asked.

Jacob's dad smiled and went and grabbed a shovel and they both started digging. They worked together, tearing a hole through the lawn and working their way through the dark brown dirt underneath. About a foot down under the grass, Jacob hit wood.

They pried an old wooden chest out of the ground. It was heavy and had a rusted iron latch.

Young Jacob took a deep breath before he opened it, and inside were the two things he most wanted for his birthday. A brand-new basketball and a gaming system.

Jacob watched his younger self nearly explode with happiness. He remembered how magical it was pulling two new shiny objects out of an old chest buried in the dirt. He could never figure out how his dad had managed to pull it off.

But now he knew. His dad had a time machine. He was the Timekeeper.

Sarah rested her hand on his shoulder. "Do you want to go talk to him?" she whispered.

Jacob watched his younger self give his dad a big hug and they rushed inside together to go start playing games. He turned to Sarah and shook his head.

"Not now," he said. "I don't want to change anything about that moment."

Sarah nodded and said, "Forest, May sixteenth, 2012, two p.m., warp."

Chapter 35

Sarah barely had time to adjust to being back in the forest in their neighborhood before her parents arrived. They stared silently at Sarah with their arms crossed.

The kids all froze and let go of the time machine and Mick slipped it into his pocket. Sarah glanced at her parents. Had they seen the time machine? It didn't look as if they had.

"Tell me about your feelings," Sarah's dad said to the children in greeting.

She felt an elbow from Dexter. Another one of Phil's expressions.

Sarah's dad cleared his throat. "Sarah, come with us, please. Now."

It gave her a chill when she realized he wasn't looking at her when he said it. He was looking at Mick Cracken.

Even more troublesome, Mick Cracken was meeting his gaze with a fiery stare of his own. He didn't appear to be intimidated in the slightest by the appearance of angry grown-ups.

Sarah slumped over toward her parents. "Stand up straight, young lady," her mom said with a cool voice.

Sarah righted her spine. She had to wait for a moment while her parents gave one last stare at Jacob, Mick, Catalina, and Dexter before they turned and walked toward home. Sarah followed, wishing with all her might that she didn't have to obey.

A swirl of emotions stirred within Sarah as she walked behind her parents. The indignity of having to leave Jacob behind just because her parents said so. The fact that she knew her parents didn't approve of Jacob. There was something about the strange stare her mom had given Catalina and that her dad had given Mick that set her on edge. She wondered what they knew, about space and about Catalina and Mick.

She briefly thought of the Strangers, but she pushed the thought from her mind.

There's no way her parents could be Strangers. Could they?

When they arrived home, Sarah went and grabbed

a banana from the fruit basket and started to walk upstairs when she caught her dad staring at a message on his phone. He showed it to Sarah's mom and her eyes widened.

They were startled when they noticed that Sarah had seen them, but they quickly regained their composure.

"Darling, we have to leave for a few hours," Sarah's dad said.

"And you are not to step foot outside the premises," her mom said.

"Not one foot," her dad said.

"When we return, I expect you to have practiced the piano for at least an hour," her mom said.

"And do not try to skimp on the time," her dad said. "You know we are able to tell the difference."

Sarah's throat felt dry and scratchy and she just nodded. She didn't want to practice the piano. She wanted to escape and go back out and find Jacob Wonderbar. But she was too scared of her parents to risk that.

When her parents closed the door behind them, Sarah trudged upstairs for a brief nap. She passed the door to her parents' room, and her nagging doubts returned. Could they really be mixed up with the Strangers?

As if pulled by an invisible force, she turned and walked toward her parents' bedroom. She paused at the door. She was strictly forbidden from entering her parents' room without their permission, but she slowly turned the doorknob and walked inside. Her heart raced as she padded across their thick carpet, walking slowly toward the closet. She knew from previous surreptitious snooping sessions that her parents had a locked compartment inside.

She had also seen her mom hiding the key in the corner of the room one time when she didn't know Sarah was home. Sarah had never had the courage to see what was behind that door, but now she had to know why her parents knew about Mick and Catalina. Some part of her thought the answer was behind the locked door.

She walked to the corner of the room, carefully peeled back the carpet in the corner, and sure enough, the key was there. She grabbed it quickly.

She thought she heard a noise and whipped her head around. She pressed her ear to the floor to see if she could hear if her mom had returned. No one was there.

Heart pounding, she climbed slowly into the closet, which was dark and smelled like her parents. Their clothes hovered around her. She took a deep breath,

slipped the key into the lock, and opened the door.

She saw black robes. Trembling, she grabbed one of the hangers and pulled on it. A necklace with a gold triangle tumbled onto the floor of the closet. Sarah burst into tears.

Her parents were Strangers.

Chapter 36

Jacob didn't have the heart to keep fighting Mick for the time machine after Sarah left. He let him walk away with it. Dexter and Catalina did the same. The four of them stood staring at one another in the forest.

Jacob trusted Mick less than ever, but with only one time machine, there was only one option. "All right, Mick," Jacob said. "We need to work together."

Mick nodded, the edge of his lips curling into a half smile, half sneer. "Glad to see you coming around."

When Jacob had warped them back to his birthday, he hadn't really thought it through—he'd just named the first date that came to mind. And when he arrived, he had simply absorbed the whole scene. He didn't want to ruin that perfect moment by talking to his dad.

But it had given him an idea. Now he knew exactly where and when he wanted to warp. And he needed Mick's help to do it.

"Listen," Jacob said. "I want to—"

He didn't have time to finish. They were suddenly face-to-face with Luger Smythe and Chloe Daisy, who had warped into the clearing.

Luger was wearing a black robe, and a belt that held a long, thin sword with a twirling golden handle. Chloe looked simultaneously worried and satisfied.

"I must apologize," Luger said, caressing the ornate hilt of his rapier. "I didn't have time to arrange an elephant."

Jacob felt a slap on his shoulder. Mick held up his time machine and beckoned Jacob to back up. Catalina ducked behind Mick and looked extremely worried.

Jacob wondered why, if Luger already had a time machine, he hadn't just gone and stopped the Astral spaceship from taking off and putting an end to everything. But he had a feeling that it had every-thing to do with the small key in Mick's hand. As long as there was another time machine in existence, someone could go back and fix things. Nothing was permanent.

If Luger was going to defeat Astrals once and for all, he needed both time machines. And as Jacob backed

away, he knew that Mick was thinking the exact same thing.

"Who is this guy?" Dexter asked.

"It's Luger Smythe," Mick said. "And he wants to get rid of Astrals."

"But . . ." Dexter said. "Why?"

Luger grinned and a chilly breeze stirred the forest. He pointed at Mick. "This alien spawn does not want you to know that their scientists predicted that Astrals would someday surpass Earth humans and rule the entire universe. Earth would be destroyed. Their own scientists have foreseen it."

Dexter turned to Mick. "Is that true?"

Jacob waited for Mick to refute Luger's allegations, but instead Mick paused and shuffled his feet. "Mick?" Jacob asked.

Mick took out a handkerchief and blew his nose. "Um. Technically, yes."

Jacob turned on Mick. "Wait, what?"

Mick rolled his eyes and mumbled, "Some of our scientists predicted that Astrals would destroy Earth. You heard him. But nothing is certain."

Jacob remembered his last trip to space, how he had narrowly escaped Patrick Gravy and the SEERs, who had tried to kidnap him and had Earth in their crosshairs. Jacob and Mick had barely stopped them

from blowing up Earth. Now he wondered if Mick was playing a longer game. Maybe that was why he was being so secretive and keeping Jacob from finding his father. Maybe Mick wasn't so opposed to blowing up Earth after all if it meant defeating the Strangers.

"Grab on," Mick muttered without moving his lips, tilting the time machine ever so slightly. Jacob noticed that Catalina was already discreetly holding on to her brother's shirt.

Jacob turned back to Luger Smythe. He was certainly creepy-looking, but maybe he wasn't wrong about everything. Maybe Astrals were dangerous after all. He couldn't shake the feeling that he might be helping Mick in some nefarious plot that he still didn't understand.

But even though Mick was conniving and a liar and Jacob knew he would never change, deep down in his gut he trusted him more than Luger. Jacob may have been making a big mistake, but he decided to team up with Mick.

They needed to act quickly. He had to get Dexter's attention so they could warp.

Dexter was looking in between Luger and Mick and Chloe, pausing uncertainly.

Jacob knew they didn't have time. He ran over and grabbed Dexter by the collar, but he resisted for just

a moment. It cost them dearly. Jacob lost his grip and stumbled back, and in that moment Luger whipped out his rapier and in a dangerous arc brought it down into the air between Jacob and Dexter.

Jacob backed into Mick, who shouted, "Mick Jr., now, warp!"

Dexter was left alone in the clearing with Luger and Chloe. Luger smiled and pointed his rapier directly at Dexter's heart.

Chloe shrieked. "What are you doing to him?"

Luger ran the rapier slowly over Dexter's head. Dexter trembled, not sure what to do and very nervous that Luger would stick it straight through him.

"He is friends with the aliens and I intend to take him prisoner," Luger said, resting his sword on Dexter's shoulder. "When they come back for him, I shall be ready."

Chapter 37

Sarah collapsed onto her bed and pounded her pillow.

It wasn't true, she thought to herself. It couldn't be true. But there was no mistaking what she had found in her parents' closets. The black robes. The same triangle necklaces that she had seen on the scary Stranger in the Palais des Tuileries.

She wanted to think it was a coincidence or a mistake or even a Halloween costume, but deep down she knew it was real. It explained so much. How her parents always forbade her to spend time with Jacob. How her mom had once been friends with Dexter's mom but had apparently had a falling out. How they both had seemed to recognize Mick and Catalina. She didn't know how or why her parents had descended into something so frightening and awful, but some part of their mysterious behavior now made sense. Maybe her parents weren't as concerned with Jacob's behavior as they were with the fact that he was half Astral.

"Sarah?" she heard a meek voice say from her doorway.

It was Chloe.

"You!" Sarah shouted. She sat up quickly and was ready to attack her sister, but when she saw Chloe's face, her rage evaporated.

Tears were streaming down Chloe's cheeks and her eyes were wide with terror. She didn't look like an annoying and larger-than-life ten-year-old who somehow made herself seem taller through force of will; she looked like a small, scared girl. All of her bravado and brattiness had been replaced with sadness and fear.

"I'm sorry," Chloe sobbed. "I'm so sorry. I messed everything up and now Dexter . . ." She started crying again.

Sarah's heart skipped a beat. "What happened to Dexter?"

"Luger Smythe has him!" Chloe said. "He won't let him go, he's trying to trap Mick and Jacob. My poor Dexy!"

Chloe walked to Sarah's bed, tipped over, and slammed her face in the covers. Even under the circumstances, Sarah couldn't help but chuckle at how dramatic her sister was. She reached over and patted Chloe on the back.

"Why, Chlo, why? Why did you give him the time machine?"

Chloe sat up and narrowed her eyes at Sarah. But then she seemed to remember herself and relented. "I heard Mom and Dad talking. One night, I was sneaking around because I was bored and I heard them talking about space people and a time machine and someone called Luger Smythe and how they had to get him one so he could stop space people from destroying Earth. They seemed so scared and it all sounded really important. So when you guys showed up with time machines, I wanted to do it myself."

"But Chlo . . . you're ten! Why didn't you . . ."

"You always say that!" Chloe shouted, all of her fire suddenly back. "You never let me go anywhere and you always treat me like a stupid little kid."

Sarah was taken aback, mainly because she was usually the one complaining that people were treating her like a silly little girl. She wanted to dismiss what Chloe was saying and chalk it up to further evidence of brattiness, but when Sarah thought about it for a

moment, she realized Chloe did have a point, as much as it pained Sarah to admit it. She wasn't always nice to Chloe when she wanted to come along with her. She corrected herself: She was rarely nice to Chloe when she wanted to come along with her. Was she ever nice to Chloe when she wanted to come along with her?

"I'm sorry," Sarah said. "You're right. I'm not always nice. It's just hard being an older sister. Sometimes I want to be with my friends and I need that to be okay. You would want the same thing if you were me. But . . . I'll try to be nicer." Sarah closed her eyes and steeled her resolve. "And you can come along with me sometimes. Once in a while. If I approve it in advance."

Chloe nodded and seemed satisfied.

"But Chlo, those are really bad people. You don't know what you're mixed up in. They want to kill Jacob. And all kinds of other people. They're scary and dangerous and mean."

Chloe winced and nodded. "I know that now. I do. Luger is really, really weird. But why would Mom and Dad want to help people who are scary and dangerous?"

Sarah wasn't sure she could answer that question and it gnawed at her. She didn't know. She loved her parents and it was terrifying to find out that they could be involved in something so strange. She was so used to doing what her parents said and going along with their orders, she hadn't ever stopped to consider they might be wrong about something. That maybe they had dark sides that Sarah had never before seen clearly.

"I think our parents are mixed up with bad people," Sarah said.

Chloe started crying again, and Sarah cried too and grabbed her sister and hugged her.

"But that doesn't mean we're bad people," Sarah whispered.

Chapter 38

Catalina grabbed Jacob's hand when they were safely aboard the spaceship Mick Jr.

"Darling, I'm so glad we're finally together," she said, batting her eyelashes. "Why don't we go somewhere and talk?"

Jacob let go of her hand and grabbed Mick by the shirt instead. "We have to go back for Dexter."

Mick looked down at Jacob's clenched hand.

"Mick Jr.?" Mick said, still looking at Jacob's hand. "A cup of tea, please."

"With pleasure," Mick Jr. answered.

A tray emerged from the wall holding a small black saucer with steaming tea. Mick grabbed it and slurped a sip, grimacing at the bitterness.

"Ah," Mick said. "That's nice."

Jacob released Mick's shirt but kept staring daggers at him. He was prepared for all of Mick's traps this time. He wouldn't be distracted. He wouldn't let Mick warp without him. He wouldn't fall for any of Mick's lies. He would be in charge.

"We have to go back," Jacob said, his voice firm and even.

Mick shook his head. "No."

"Yes."

"I'm disappointed in you," Mick said, taking another sip of tea.

"Darling," Catalina said, grabbing Jacob's hand again. "Wouldn't you like to spend some time catching up? I have so much to tell you."

"No. We're going back," Jacob said.

Mick set the saucer of tea back on the tray and it disappeared with a faint hiss. "It's a trap. A hostage situation. We'll never win."

Jacob realized how little he knew about Luger's power. He had only seen Luger and Chloe in the forest, but for all he knew, Luger could have warped an entire medieval army into the forest, just waiting to trap them and steal the time machine. Luger may have known not to tip his hand ahead of time. If Jacob and Mick warped straight back to the forest, they might fall right into Luger's trap.

"There," Mick said. "You understand. Care for a cup of tea? Mick Jr. makes a mean Earl Grey."

"The best in the universe," Mick Jr. said.

Jacob turned around and walked away without answering. He needed time to think.

"Jakey, darling," Catalina said as she caught him on the way.

"Not now!" Jacob shouted. He winced at her pained expression and felt a wave of guilt. He always found himself being rude to her.

"Sorry," he said. "Yeah, you can come with me. Just not him." He jerked his finger back at Mick.

Catalina clapped happily.

"And hey, Mick Jr.?" Jacob said. "If you listen in on Catalina and me, I'm going to paint you purple from nose to fin."

Mick Jr. was silent for a moment. "I'm still smarter than you," he said.

"And please make me a chocolate milk," Jacob said.

Jacob thought he felt the ship shudder. "With extreme . . . displeasure. Sir."

A tray emerged from the wall and Jacob took a sip of the chocolate milk. It was actually pretty good.

Jacob and Catalina walked into one of the staterooms and Jacob shut the door. The sheets on the bed were orange and Jacob wondered if Mick Jr. had

changed them for him knowing it was his favorite color. Or maybe it was a trap and he would be captured if he went near the bed. He sat down in one of the chairs in the room to be on the safe side. Catalina took a seat opposite of him.

He braced himself for what she was going to say. He knew she had a crush on him no matter how much he resisted her, and he found it rather exasperating. The word *no* was not in Catalina's vocabulary. It never occurred to her that anything she had her mind set on was not completely possible and within her grasp. It was one of the things Jacob admired about her, but it meant he always had to keep his distance. He looked away so as not to give her any ideas.

"What did you want to talk to me about?" Jacob mumbled.

"Us!" Catalina said.

Jacob sighed. It was worse than he feared. She wasn't usually so direct. "Catalina . . ."

"Do you know why I like you, Jakey?" Catalina asked.

Jacob averted his eyes and stared at the floor. "Why?"

Catalina held out her hand. He didn't reach for hers, so she scooted closer and took his hand anyway.

"It's not because you're handsome, even though

you're very handsome. It's not because you're fun, even though you're very, very fun. It's not because you're tough, even though you are."

Jacob's face felt warm and he hoped he wasn't blushing.

"It's because you're confident, Jakey. You can do anything and you know it."

Jacob blinked. He had never thought about himself that way. In fact, he had always thought Catalina was the confident one. She seemed like she knew she could do anything. Was he the same way? Was that how other people saw him? Maybe he and Catalina had more in common than he had thought.

"Thanks," he said, and this time he looked her in the eye when he said it.

Catalina smiled. "And I have something for you."

Jacob couldn't imagine what she wanted to give him, and he tried to tease out the meaning of her facial expression.

She took out a key. It looked like . . .

"It's the third time machine," she said. "I've been trying to give it to you this whole time."

She handed it over to him and he ran his fingers over its rough outlines. It almost felt rusted and yet it possessed unlimited power. He didn't have to steal Mick's time machine. He didn't have to try and

outsmart Luger to get the one Chloe had lost. He could go anywhere and do anything, thanks to Catalina.

"Thanks," Jacob said, though he couldn't help but hesitate. "Are you sure you want to give it to me?"

Catalina squeezed his hand. "Go find your dad," she said.

Jacob knew where he wanted to warp. He finally had a plan. He wasn't sure it would solve everything, but for the first time since he had heard his dad was missing, he knew exactly what he wanted to do.

But he couldn't go there yet. He turned the time machine over in his hand.

"Thank you, Catalina. I will find my dad," he said. He slipped the time machine into his pocket. "But first I have to save Dexter."

Chapter 39

Sarah squeezed Chloe's shoulder in terror when she heard the front door open.

"Ow!" Chloe yelped.

"Shh," Sarah whispered.

There were footsteps downstairs. Their parents were home.

"Tell me about your feelings?" Sarah's dad called out.

"Sarah? Chloe?" Sarah's mom said. "Please come downstairs."

"This instant," Sarah's dad said.

Sarah and Chloe locked eyes and didn't move.

"What do we do?" Chloe asked.

Sarah didn't know. Her life had been upended.

Before, the sound of her parents coming home would have seemed comfortable, familiar, even exciting. Now she was scared of them and didn't know if she could trust them. Sarah knew deep down that they loved her, but she felt torn. They most definitely did not want what was best for Jacob Wonderbar and Mick and all the Astrals she had grown to care about. They were still her parents, but she knew in her heart of hearts that they were wrong.

"We have to find Jacob," Sarah whispered. "He'll know what to do."

Chloe nodded. There was fear in her eyes, but Sarah also saw appreciation. They were a team now, and instead of feeling like Chloe was a little flea on her back, always biting and making her life miserable, she felt protective of her instead. Chloe was her little sister, and two Daisys working together were a powerful force indeed.

Sarah heard the footsteps on the stairs.

"Sarah?" her mom said.

"Chloe?" her dad said.

There was a rattle at the door handle and suddenly Sarah's parents were in the doorway. She had spent the last hour thinking of them as monsters, but when she saw them standing in her doorway, it was easy to think that everything was normal, that it had been a misunderstanding, that those robes in the closet were just Halloween costumes after all.

But she shook those thoughts out of her head. Sarah knew what she had seen. Her parents really were involved in something bad, and it was up to her and her friends to put a stop to it. She couldn't imagine her life without Astrals, especially without Jacob.

Sarah squeezed Chloe's hand twice.

"What's wrong, darlings?" Sarah's mom asked.

Sarah steadied herself. She needed to think clearly.

"It's time we talked to you girls about something," Sarah's dad said.

"Something . . . dangerous," Sarah's mom said.

"We don't want to alarm you," Sarah's dad said. "But it is extremely important that you stay away from Jacob Wonderbar."

"And all of his friends," her mom said.

"Girls, you know how some people think there are aliens out there? All those UFO sightings and legends and things?"

"Those things are true," her mom said.

Her dad nodded. "There are aliens, and they are very, very dangerous. They are extremely powerful. And they mean us harm."

"Isn't that terrible?" her mom asked.

"Nothing is going to happen now, we're not in immediate danger, but you must listen to us."

"You must stay away from Jacob Wonderbar."

"You two girls are the most important things in the universe to your mom and me," her dad said. "You're the light of our lives."

"We want to protect you," her mom said.

"And we know how scary this must be to you. Trust your mother and me," her dad said.

"Stay away from Jacob Wonderbar."

"This will all be over soon," her dad said.

"*Very* soon," her mom said.

Sarah knew her parents might have meant well, and they were partly right that Astrals were dangerous to Earth. But her parents and the Strangers were just as bad as the SEERs. They had taken everything too far.

Sarah shuddered at the idea that it could all be over soon, with the Strangers winning and Astrals never existing in the first place and Jacob Wonderbar never being born.

Sarah started to cry, and her parents enveloped her in a hug.

"There, there," Sarah's mom said.

"We'll take care of this," Sarah's dad said.

"You have to trust us," Sarah's mom said.

Sarah pulled away from her parents and looked them in the eye.

"We found a time machine," Sarah said.

Her parents tried not to show their surprise, and they exchanged a quick glance. "You don't . . . Where is it?" her dad asked.

Sarah pointed at her desk. "It's in the top drawer."

Sarah's dad nodded and went to go investigate. That left only her mom standing in the way of escape.

Chloe looked out the window and gasped in horror.

"What is it?" her mom asked, and she leaned over to peer outside.

Chloe grabbed Sarah's hand and they ran for the door. Sarah felt her mom grasp the smallest end of her shirt, but she broke away and they rushed through the door and down the stairs.

"Girls!" her dad shouted. "Come back this instant!"

His shout had an almost magnetic pull on Sarah and she hesitated. She couldn't remember ever disobeying her parents, certainly nothing as dramatic as running away from them when they were shouting at her to return. But it was Chloe who was the confident one, and as she pulled insistently on Sarah's hand, Sarah relented and kept running.

They threw open the front door and ran down the

dirt path in the direction of Jacob's house. Darkness had fallen on their street and Sarah risked a glance back over her shoulder, but she didn't see her parents or Dexter or Luger Smythe or any of the Strangers.

Sarah and Chloe reached Jacob's house. She hoped that he had somehow escaped Luger, but he wasn't there and her heart rose into her throat. What if he was in deep trouble? She was just about to pound on

Mrs. Wonderbar's door when Mick, Catalina, and Jacob materialized on the front lawn.

Sarah yelped in surprise when she saw Jacob, and she didn't know whether to hug him or punch him for scaring her.

So she did both.

Chapter 40

We can't go charging into the forest," Mick said.

Jacob, Sarah, Chloe, Catalina, and Mick sat huddled in a circle behind a tall bush in a yard a few houses down from Jacob's house. The night was dark and chilly and every shadow held the specter of a Stranger lurking, ready to snatch the children away and put an end to everything they were fighting for. The breeze ominously stirred the trees, and the children darted their eyes around, each taking responsibility for keeping watch.

"We go straight into the forest, that's certain death," Mick said.

Jacob nodded. Mick was right. The Strangers were expecting them, and charging in was far too dangerous. Who knew what traps awaited them? Jacob and Mick were unarmed, and even though they could have warped straight to the Planet Valkyrie armory and stolen all of Patrick Gravy's finest blasters, Jacob knew it was too dangerous to add weapons into the mix. It was bad enough that there were swords involved. Very sharp and pointy swords, Jacob thought with a gulp.

Mick held out the time machine. "Where should we go?"

It was quiet for a moment, but Jacob spoke up. "We go back to the 1500s. To stop Chloe from giving Luger the time machine."

Jacob shrugged at Chloe. She just stared at the grass.

"Jake, there's something you should know," Sarah said. "The reason Chloe gave the time machine to Luger is because my parents are Strangers."

Jacob recoiled. "Your parents?"

"I know," Sarah said. "It's terrible."

Jacob thought about all the times he had been over at Sarah's house and how they had treated him with such suspicion. He had never felt comfortable around them, and he wondered if it was because they knew he was half Astral. He tried to wrap his mind around what it meant.

"It's time," Mick said. He tipped the key in Chloe's direction. Jacob placed his hand on top of it, then

Sarah, then Catalina. Chloe pressed her lips together and placed her hand on top of Catalina's.

"We can do this," Jacob said. "For Dexter."

"For Dexter," the others repeated.

"Tower of London, Luger Smythe's office, July sixteenth, 1525, four p.m.," Chloe said. "Warp!"

The air was sucked out of Jacob's lungs and when he opened his eyes, he was back in the Tower of London, which he smelled before he even fully got his bearings. Chloe and Luger were in front of him and she was just about to hand over the key.

"No!" present-Chloe shouted from Jacob's right. "Don't do it!"

Past Chloe paused, but Luger wrenched away the key. They had mistimed their warp. They needed to go back five minutes earlier.

Jacob felt something very sharp jab his back. He turned around and royal guards with spears filled the hallway outside the office. Dexter peeked around from behind them.

"Warp! Warp!" Dexter shouted. "It's a trap!"

Jacob was furious. He should have known Luger would guess that they'd try to stop him from getting his hands on the time machine. It wouldn't do any good to go farther back in time, either. The guards would be waiting. The children touched one another's shoulders.

"Where do we go?!" Sarah shouted.

"Forest by our house, May sixteenth, 2012, eight p.m., warp!" Jacob shouted as fast as he could.

The air rushed out of his lungs and when he opened his eyes in the forest he saw more guards. Luger had thought of everything. And sure enough, Luger and Dexter warped into the clearing just after Jacob and his friends. One soldier raised a fearsome battle-axe and began swinging it down in the direction of the time machine.

"Numonia, now, warp!" Jacob shouted.

When Jacob opened his eyes, he saw nothing but gray and his nose pricked with the familiar smell of burp breath. He saw a glint of silver on the horizon and he began bounding toward the spaceship Swift. Sarah, Catalina, and Mick followed close behind. Jacob heard a shout and saw Luger Smythe and four soldiers warp onto the tiny dustball of a planet. They struggled to bounce along, unused to the planet's weak gravity, but eventually they used their larger strides to nearly catch up with the children.

As Jacob neared the ship, night fell and a chill swept over the planet. He could see the barest glint of the spaceship Swift and held on to Sarah, Catalina, and

Mick as they walked toward it. When the sun rose, they were face-to-face with Moonman McGillicutty, who for some reason was digging a hole with a large shovel.

"Jacob Wonderbar! Sarah Daisy! I knew you'd come back, I just knew it!" Moonman shouted, giving them a big hug. Then he saw Mick Cracken and Catalina, and his face grew serious. He sniffed and said, "Mr. President. Madame Vice President." He tried to say it politely, but his distaste was palpable. He hadn't forgiven Mick for beating Jacob in the presidential election.

"We're in trouble!" Jacob shouted. "Those soldiers are trying to get us. Can you help us stop them?"

Moonman clutched his shovel and clapped Jacob on the shoulder. "Don't you worry about a thing."

Moonman set off running in the direction of the soldiers.

"Wait!" Jacob shouted. When he had asked for help he was not remotely envisioning that Moonman would try to take on four soldiers with nothing but a shovel. But Moonman bounded toward them, cocking the shovel behind him like a baseball bat.

The soldiers stopped in alarm. Just when Moonman was about to reach them, night came and Moonman fell fast asleep.

212

In the soft light Jacob could see Moonman immobile on the horizon, holding the shovel over his shoulder. The soldiers stepped over to him and waved in his face, not quite sure what was happening. Then they left him alone and started running toward the children again.

"Grab on," Mick whispered, and Jacob, Sarah, Catalina, and Mick made sure they were grasping one another's shoulders, just as the sun was rising. "Planet Royale Courtyard, now, warp," he said as quietly as he possibly could.

They arrived in the Planet Royale Courtyard, filled with festive topiaries cut in the shape of animals and spaceships, and they braced themselves to see if they had been quiet enough to escape Luger's pursuit. If he didn't hear where they had warped, they could regroup and come up with a new plan.

But sure enough, it was only seconds before Luger Smythe and his soldiers warped into the courtyard. Jacob felt his shoulders slump in defeat.

"How did they know?" Jacob asked Mick.

Mick's expression was grim. "They have all the time in the world to find us. How many places did you check before this one?" he asked Luger.

"This was the third," Luger said, his accent crisp and precise. "I didn't ever expect you to be quite this foolish."

The soldiers circled around and the kids were too exhausted to make a run for it.

"We have to warp!" Sarah muttered. "Now."

"No," Mick said, pulling away from Jacob, Sarah, and Catalina. "This ends here."

Jacob's heart sank. This wasn't the time for Mick to play the hero. They had to keep running to stay out of Luger's grasp. They had to save Dexter. He thought about pulling out his own time machine and warping, but Catalina caught his eye and shook her head quickly. Jacob knew she was right. It was too risky to reveal he had it.

"Astrals are peaceful," Mick said, walking confidently up to Luger and staring him right in the eye. "We are good people. We have our crazies just like any other group of people, but we mean Earth no harm."

"Not likely," Luger spat.

Mick pressed on. Jacob had the feeling Mick had rehearsed this speech before, but like everything else with his quest to defeat the Strangers, Jacob suspected it hadn't been entirely thought through. "My ancestors set out into the stars so that we could have a better life, so we could live in peace and do what we love. And that's exactly what we did. It's called *joie de vivre*. It's beautiful. The greatest moment in my entire life was when I became the leader of this incredible civilization."

Luger paused for a moment, considering what Mick was saying. He nodded at his guards, who stepped forward and grabbed Sarah and Catalina by the shoulders. Jacob was quick enough to back away from the guard who gave him pursuit. He feinted and kept the soldier off balance, knowing everything would be lost if he was captured. He hoped Mick could talk his way out of this one.

"Look at me," Mick said, spreading his arms wide and smiling. "I'm unarmed. I'm not calling the guards. I'm here in peace. Let's end this once and for all."

Luger smiled. Then, before Jacob could react, Luger whipped out his rapier, swung it in a blinding arc, and brought it down with a crack on Mick's wrist. Mick's time machine clattered away on the stone steps of the court-

yard. He yelped in pain and crumpled to the ground. Sarah and Catalina screamed.

"No!" Jacob shouted.

Jacob saw a thin line of blood seeping through Mick's sleeve as he rolled around on the ground, groaning in pain. It wasn't a mortal wound and Jacob realized Luger must have hit him with the flat edge of the blade.

Luger stepped over and picked up Mick's time machine. He tossed it to the guard who held Sarah, who touched gloves with the guard grasping Catalina. "Tower of London prison, July sixteenth, one p.m., 1525, warp!"

They were gone. Jacob had lost Sarah again.

Luger stood over Mick, savoring his victory. He gave one last glare at Jacob. "We're not finished, alien." He touched a boot to Mick's stomach and said, "Tower of London dungeon, July sixteenth, one p.m., 1525. Warp."

Jacob was alone.

Chapter 41

Jacob walked to the edge of the lagoon in the courtyard of Planet Royale, marveling at the silence all
around him. Mortimer, the talkative small pink dol-
phin, swooped into the air and said "Hi!" The most
Jacob could do was wave. Mortimer seemed satisfied.

He didn't know why Luger had taken everyone but
him. He wondered if Luger somehow didn't consider
him a threat or if there was one last, dangerous trap
still awaiting him. The Strangers hadn't succeeded in
stopping the Astrals from blasting off yet, otherwise
Jacob wouldn't even be alive, but he wondered how
much time he had left before Luger won. There wasn't
much Jacob could do to protect the Astrals now.

He didn't know where to turn.

Suddenly the king of the universe, or rather the former king of the universe, was standing beside him. Jacob had been so distracted staring off on the horizon, he hadn't noticed the king approach.

"These are dark times," the king said.

It was an understatement. Jacob couldn't imagine how the times could have been any darker. Sarah and Dexter and Catalina were captured. Mick was hurt. An entire magical civilization was in danger of being wiped from history. It was life and death on a massive scale, and Jacob felt the weight of it all resting on his shoulders. He was second-guessing every decision that had led him to this grave predicament. He should have gotten help earlier, he should have talked to the king, he should have tried harder to find his dad. He had tried to do everything himself and he had made a mess of everything. He should have realized Mick's plan to take on the Strangers himself would never work.

He turned to the king. "What do I do?"

He needed some answers. He needed direction. He didn't want to have to figure things out for himself anymore.

The king clapped him on the shoulder. "Jacob, what you need to know about dark times is that they end. It may feel as if hope is lost, that there's nothing left to fight for. But it is precisely at the moment when

218

all hope seems lost that you must remember to hope again."

Jacob took in the words, but he still felt deflated. The king wasn't going to give him the answers. He wanted Jacob to solve things on his own.

Jacob wanted to go back and fix everything. He didn't just want to stop his friends from being captured by Strangers, he wanted more than that. He had spent so much time in space looking for his dad and hoping that he would see him, but for every bit he had hoped, he had experienced even greater heartbreak. Getting his hopes up had left him feeling worse than if he had never hoped at all.

What he really wanted was for his dad to have never left in the first place.

If his dad had just never left, none of it would have ever happened. Jacob wouldn't be alone and grasping for any idea how to save his friends. His dad would have known what to do. Everything wouldn't have all been resting on Jacob's shoulders.

The king patted Jacob on the back. "Your hope will make you strong."

Jacob clenched his jaw. He knew what he had to do. It was time to set things right. From the very beginning.

"Why did you make my dad the Timekeeper?" Jacob asked. "He can't even change a car tire."

The king smiled faintly and said, "You underestimate your father. We all have different talents. Your father's talent is that he cannot be corrupted by the temptations of time travel."

Jacob wasn't sure he understood what that meant, but he took out the time machine and held it up.

"Be strong," the king said.

Jacob stared at the time machine and steeled his nerves. "May fifth, 2010, eight p.m., lawn outside my house. Warp."

The air rushed out of Jacob's lungs and he found himself staring at his house. The air was warm, the evening was peaceful, and the setting sun turned the sky pink above the forest down the street.

It was the night Jacob's dad left for good. It was the night when Jacob Wonderbar's life had changed forever.

Jacob took a deep breath and started walking toward the door. He had never had a chance to stop his dad from leaving that night. But this time he would convince him not to leave. He would stop his dad from walking out the door. He would make him turn around, go back inside, and be a dad. Jacob's entire life would be different. Better. He would continue to have exciting birthdays and dangerous camping trips,

and he wouldn't spend the next two years wondering when he would ever see his dad again.

He would stop his dad on their front porch. And Jacob would have the life he wanted.

"Jacob," he heard a voice behind him say. "Wait."

His breath caught and he turned around.

It was his dad. Not his dad from the night he left home, but his current dad, a few years older, a little grayer, with the same friendly eyes and fidgety feet. The dad he had thought about every day. The dad he had traveled billions of miles through space and thousands of years through time trying to find.

The dad he had been waiting to see for the last two years.

Chapter 42

"Dad . . ."

"Hello, son."

Jacob blinked up at his dad. Over the years he had rehearsed so many different variations of what he would say the moment he found him. There was the version where he pushed his dad in his chest and told him how mad he was and berated him for leaving. There was the version where he tried to be patient and waited for his dad to explain what had happened, because there had to be a good explanation for everything. There was the version where he hugged him and immediately forgave him and was just happy that they were reunited. There was the version where he stormed off without saying a single word.

But now that he was seeing the real thing, face-to-face with his dad, he felt completely frozen. He didn't know what to do. He wanted to push, hug, yell, cry, and run away all at once.

His dad acted first and pulled Jacob into a hug. Jacob accepted the hug but kept his eyes open, staring off into the twilight.

"What are you doing here?" Jacob asked.

Jacob's dad let him go but kept his hands on Jacob's shoulders. He gave Jacob a chagrined half smile. "Mick Cracken stranded me here," he said.

Jacob frowned. "But Mick said he . . ." He didn't have to finish. Mick had lied about where he had stranded his dad. He wanted to throw Jacob off the chase.

"That boy has a truth problem," his dad said, shaking his head. "I can't believe I fell for it."

"What happened between you two?"

Jacob's dad tapped his foot. "When Mick became president, he and I had different ideas about how to deal with the Strangers. He thought he could take on Luger Smythe himself. He knew it was my job to stop people from interfering with the past, and if they did interfere with the past, it was my duty to go back and fix what they changed. So he stranded me in time to keep me from stopping him. He probably told you I was somewhere else in time to throw you off the scent. I've been stuck here a week."

Jacob felt a fresh wave of anger at Mick. Another lie from the universe's ultimate liar. But he didn't want to be talking about Mick and his beef with his dad and what to do with the Strangers.

"Where have you been?!" Jacob asked, anger creeping into his voice. "Why didn't you show up when you said you would?"

Jacob's heart raced and he realized how mad he was. He thought about the humiliation of waiting for his dad for hours when he received the postcard and feeling stupid for thinking he would show. He thought about all those times his dad could have called or written or just shown up.

"I have a really difficult job, Jacob," his dad said. "Astrals are always making homemade time machines and messing with the past, and I have to go back and confiscate them and set things right again. I mean, look at our street," he said, waving at the jungle outside of Jacob's house. "This isn't the way this neighborhood is supposed to look. I can only imagine what else Mick has done. It could take a very long time to fix everything."

"But . . ." Jacob sputtered. "You haven't been lost this whole time?"

His dad averted his eyes and looked very sad. "Jacob, I wish I could tell you I was lost or that there was some reason why I didn't come back. I wish there was something I could say to make everything better. But there's not a simple explanation. I wanted to come back. Something just . . . kept getting in the way. There was always a new problem to fix. Maybe I was scared too. I had been gone for so long . . ."

"So you're too busy stopping Astral pranks to come to my basketball games? I thought you had a time machine."

His dad turned his eyes to Jacob. "It's complicated, Jacob. I can't just go back in time to change my mistakes. I'm the Timekeeper. The past has to stay in the past. Everything depends on it. It's the reason the king chose me. He knew that no matter how many regrets I had about my life, I wouldn't try to change the way things happened. I have to live with my own mistakes no matter how difficult that is for me. I have to live by example, or it would mean chaos for everyone." He waved his hand at the trees. "I mean, look at this mess. It could be far worse than this."

Jacob's eyes welled with tears. He couldn't believe what he was hearing. He had pictured his dad being

stranded by strange Astrals or stuck behind a supernova explosion or trying desperately but unsuccessfully to reach him. But none of it was true. His dad hadn't been lost at all. Jacob didn't care about how much of a big shot his dad was in space. He should have been there for Jacob.

Jacob's dad sighed. "I know I haven't been a great dad. I haven't even *been* a dad at all these last few years. I don't even know what I can say except that I'm sorry."

Jacob clenched his teeth. He had come up with all those different explanations for why his father had been missing, but he instead was hearing the worst possible explanation. He wasn't lost in space. He hadn't been lost in time for the past two years. Instead he hadn't wanted to come back. Or was too much of a coward.

Jacob felt a tear drop down his face, and he wiped it away angrily. His dad tried to reach for his shoulders, but Jacob pushed his hands away. He surprised himself with his own fierceness, but tears kept welling in his eyes.

"Jacob . . ."

"Why did you leave?!" Jacob cried. "How could you have done that to me?!"

"I'm sorry," his dad said quietly. "The king asked me to—"

"Go away," Jacob said, turning back to face the door and wiping away his tears. "I don't know who you are. I'm going to fix this."

Soon his dad would emerge from the door with a suitcase in hand and Jacob would stop him. This older, cowardly version of his dad would never exist. He would stay at home and never get lost in time and wouldn't have to face any decisions about how to be a part of Jacob's life.

"Jacob . . ." his dad said again. "I can't tell you what will happen when the old me walks through that door. But think about how things will be different for you if you do stop me. Think about it."

Jacob didn't turn back. He knew how things would be different. His dad would make pancakes in the morning and take him on camping trips and make his birthdays fun. He would be there when Jacob needed advice or support or just another person he could talk to. He would be the dad that Jacob had wanted him to be.

But then Jacob thought about when he had blasted off into space the first time. Would he have had the courage to do that? He wasn't sure. He had started acting bravely mostly after his dad had left, when getting in trouble seemed like such a trifle in comparison to the hugeness of losing his dad. Whatever his

teachers or the principal could have done to punish him never felt like a big deal after that, and Jacob had experienced a newfound freedom in life. He tried to do the right thing, but it was tempting to not care as much about the consequences of his actions. His perspective had changed.

Would he have run for president of the universe? So much of his decision to run had been driven by a desire to make himself famous so his dad couldn't help but find him. If it hadn't been for his missing dad, Jacob might have declined such a big responsibility and just gone and had fun instead. He was proud of running for president, even if he had come up just short.

Jacob didn't know what would have happened if his dad hadn't left and had stayed home instead. Jacob could have gone his entire life without knowing about spaceships and time travel and places like Numonia and Planet Paisley.

Mick and Catalina and Moonman and Stargirl and the king and Praiseworthy and the crazy space monkeys and even the mean spaceship Lucy. He might never have met any of them.

Could he have passed up his life in space to keep his dad around on Earth? He still thought he might.

It had been horrible when his dad left, the worst thing he had ever experienced. He still wanted to have a dad again.

But now he wasn't sure what he should do.

Jacob's dad cleared his throat. "I haven't been a good father, Jacob. I hope you know how sorry I am. But I am so, so proud of the young man you've become."

As mad as he was, Jacob's chest warmed when he heard his dad say he was proud of him. He was proud of himself too. He turned back to face his dad.

"I've made lots of mistakes," his dad said. "And I know you've had a hard time because of me. But the past makes us who we are."

Jacob remembered how Catalina had said he was confident and how Sarah had once said she was impressed with how he had been able to move on after his dad had left. So much of what made up his personality and his strength had come as a result of the pain he had endured. He knew, as hard as it had been to experience at the time, that it had made him a better, stronger person.

But he still hesitated. The last two years had been so incredibly hard. Confidence and friendships aside, he wasn't sure it had all been worth it.

Jacob's dad said, "I need you to help me stop all this Luger Smythe madness and save the Astral people. If you go back and stop me and you're not the same kid you are now, I don't know what could happen. It could mean the end of everything for us. Mick shouldn't have tried to change the past. This isn't the way history was supposed to unfold and we need to fix this. Let me have the time machine. I need to do my job."

Jacob felt the weight of his decision pressing down on his shoulders. Did he want to stop his dad from leaving and have the childhood he deserved or did he want to be the person he had become? Did he want the friendships he had made or the father he wished for? The childhood he should have had or the Astral people he had grown to love?

It didn't seem fair that he had to choose. He wanted both. He wanted his dad and he wanted the Astrals. He wanted his friends and he wanted to be a normal kid.

But he grasped the time machine tightly and nodded to himself, knowing what he had to do. He was Jacob Wonderbar. He could do anything. He had made it through the hard times and he was strong. He felt hope again.

It was up to him to save the Astrals.

"I'm going to set things right," Jacob said. "But I'm going to do it myself."

Chapter 43

Dexter tried to ignore the rat in the corner. He had enough problems being locked up in a cell in the Tower of London where he was only fed something the guards called "gruel," a lumpy, gray, watery concoction that Dexter felt was expressly engineered to be the most unappetizing and unappealing food imaginable, even worse than the congealed space dust on Numonia. He did not need a rather disgusting roommate with a long bald tail. His only consolation was that his cell had an expansive view of the castle courtyard, and Dexter spent most of his time staring out the window at the ravens and . . .

Dexter shook his head. He must have been hallucinating. He thought he had seen a monkey scamper behind a bush.

He glanced back over his shoulder. The rat was definitely looking at him.

"Go away!" he shouted just as he thought he heard a screech in the courtyard.

Was that . . .

He looked back out at the courtyard and this time he definitely saw a monkey. It was Rufus, the small chimp Dexter had befriended his last time in space. He was wearing one of the medieval guards' helmets.

"Rufus!" Dexter shouted.

Rufus looked up and spotted Dexter and his eyes widened in recognition. He screeched in happiness.

But Rufus quickly ran away as a band of guards armed with rapiers came charging after him. He scampered around a corner and out of Dexter's sight.

"Leave him alone!" Dexter shouted.

There was a commotion in the hall outside Dexter's cell and the rat dove into a hole. Dexter heard shouts and clashes of iron and what sounded like several men being thrown against his door. Finally he heard a key in the lock and the door swung open. Dexter crouched and braced himself, unsure of what he was going to see.

It was Jacob Wonderbar. He was wearing a helmet and clutched a thin sword. And then Dexter saw Boris, the leader of the space monkeys. He chirped quietly

at Dexter, scampered over, and slapped him on the shoulder so hard, Dexter almost fell over.

"Hi, Boris!" he whispered.

Jacob ran over and pulled Dexter up. "Are you good?"

Dexter nodded. "I'm okay. Where is everyone else?"

"Sarah and Catalina are safe. Some of the monkeys are guarding them. We have to go get Mick," Jacob said. "You ready?"

Dexter nodded. He tried to steel his resolve,

especially because he knew that venturing outside his cell meant a marked increase in the likelihood he would encounter spears and swords and very mean medieval soldiers.

They ventured into the hallway, which was littered with unconscious guards who had not gotten the better of their encounter with Boris.

Jacob jerked his head toward one of them. "Want a sword?" he asked Dexter.

"Um. No thanks," Dexter said. He was not confident that he could wield a sword without stabbing himself with it.

They ran down a stone spiral staircase.

"I saw my dad," Jacob said over his shoulder.

Dexter almost tripped on one of the steps. "Your dad? As in your dad dad?"

"My dad dad," Jacob said. "I left him back in time."

"Whoa," Dexter said.

"I'll tell you about it . . ."

Boris screeched when they reached the bottom of the stairwell. Two soldiers with spears were waiting for them.

"Halt!" they shouted.

Two enraged space monkeys barreled into them from the side. They clattered to the ground in a heap and Boris bounded on top of them and gnashed his teeth.

"Good idea getting the space monkeys," Dexter said.

Jacob smiled. "They're the best."

They ran across the courtyard toward the gate that entered into the smelly river. Dexter had a feeling they were headed toward Luger Smythe's lair. And he wasn't confident they should go charging straight in, no matter how many space monkeys they had at their disposal.

"Wonderbar ... Wonderbar ..." Dexter whispered. "Are you sure this is a good idea?"

Jacob slowed. One of the ravens squawked at him.

Dexter had an idea. "Let's use the time machine," he said. "Sneak attack."

Jacob's eyes widened and he nodded. "Boris, over here," he said. Boris ambled over. They grabbed on, and Jacob warped them straight into Luger's office.

When Dexter opened his eyes, he saw Luger in the corner, the tip of his rapier pressed directly against Mick Cracken's throat.

"Drop everything," Luger said.

Dexter looked down. He didn't have anything to drop. Boris took off his helmet and let it clang to the ground. Jacob still held on tight to the time machine.

"I said *everything*," Luger said, pointing a long finger at Jacob while keeping the sword pressed against

236

Mick. "Or shall we see how much luck this alien truly possesses?"

"They know about the first Astral space launch," Mick said, his neck straining against the sword. "He got it out of me."

Dexter saw Jacob whisper to the time machine, and the next thing Dexter knew, it was Jacob, not Mick, who was facing Luger's rapier. Only he was now wearing what looked to be iron around his neck and a large chest plate.

Luger whispered to his time machine, shouted "Warp!" and suddenly Luger had a blaster pointed at Jacob's face.

Jacob whispered to his time machine, shouted "Warp!" and Luger's blaster had been replaced with a banana. Boris gasped, charged at Luger and grabbed the banana. Luger's time machine clanged to the ground. Boris began eating the banana.

Mick dove for the time machine, but Luger grabbed it just in time and held it up proudly. Catalina, Sarah, Chloe, and Rufus rushed into the room. Rufus ran over and tackled Dexter, nuzzling his face in his chest.

"Not now!" Dexter shouted.

"We've got this one!" Sarah yelled. She held up the second time machine.

But they were still in danger. Luger clutched his

time machine. Mick and Jacob circled Luger. A bead of sweat dripped down his pale face.

"You won't win," Luger said, his voice strangely calm. "I have thought of everything."

Luger whispered into his time machine, shouted "Warp!" and he was gone.

"No!" Chloe shouted.

The children stood gasping in Luger's study. Jacob threw his armor to the ground in frustration and Mick glared at the ceiling.

But gradually they all realized they were safe for the moment, and they were finally back together once again. They all rushed together and hugged one another and high-fived. Dexter did not know what he had done to deserve the greatest friends in the universe, people who were braver than him and more confident and, in the case of Sarah Daisy, far smarter than him, but he was just thankful that they were his. He was also immensely grateful he would never again have to eat gruel in his entire life.

"Where are we going to find Luger Smythe?" Sarah asked. "He still has the time machine."

Everyone looked to Jacob. Even Mick.

"There's only one place he'd go," Jacob said. "And I need Mick's help."

Chapter 44

When they got their bearings after warping, the kids were standing on a grassy hill on a chilly night looking at a magnificent, ramshackle silver spaceship. A crowd wearing 1940s clothing was buzzing with excitement, and a man with wild white hair and a reedy voice was addressing the crowd.

Sarah grabbed Jacob's hand and held it tight. "Is that Albert Einstein?" she whispered.

He nodded. She shivered a little against the cold night.

"These are the first Astrals," Jacob said quietly to Dexter and Chloe. "They're my ancestors."

"*Our* ancestors," Catalina said.

"There!" Dexter whispered. He pointed over at another hill. Jacob thought he saw a pale figure tumble over to the other side in the moonlight. It looked like Luger Smythe.

Jacob let go of Sarah's hands and crouched on the ground. He had an idea. He signaled for Mick and Catalina to go to one side of the hill. Dexter and Chloe would go around the other side. And he and Sarah would take the middle. Between the three pairs, they could keep Luger cornered. Hopefully they could sneak up on him before he warped.

Everyone nodded and they ducked down and ran into the darkness. Jacob heard Father Albert talking about the dark times they were experiencing and the better times ahead. He felt the same rush of hope, knowing that this was a crucial moment in his history, when his dad's ancestors set out to make a better life for themselves. It was an incredible thing to start a civilization built around the love of life, and he felt proud that he had come from those brave people.

Jacob and Sarah climbed slowly up the hill where they had seen Luger. When they reached the top, Jacob peeked over. He saw Dexter and Chloe on one side. Mick and Catalina on the other. And in the middle of the hill, staring straight at the spaceship, was Luger Smythe. He didn't see them coming.

Jacob charged over the hill and tackled Luger. They tumbled down the side of the hill, over and over, but

Jacob didn't let go, and when they landed with a thud at the bottom, Jacob found himself on top, with his hands locked on Luger's wrists.

"I've got you," Jacob said.

But Luger was smiling, his sharp yellow teeth glinting in the moonlight. "Do you?" he asked. "Or do *I* have *you*?"

Jacob saw the flash before he heard the noise. Suddenly it was daylight and Jacob could see for miles, then he was blown to the side by a powerful shockwave and a tremendous blast. He looked up and saw a massive fireball rising into the sky. The people in the clearing shrieked as the wreckage of the spaceship tumbled to the ground in a massive heap. The pounded metal was twisted and sharp and glowing, and what had once been a beautiful, creaky spaceship was a smoldering mess. Jacob hoped no one had been hurt.

They had lost. Jacob braced himself to disappear, to be swept into nothingness and wiped from existence. The Astrals had been stopped. The spaceship was blown to bits, the start of the Astral civilization had been prevented, and Jacob's ancestors would never be born.

But Jacob stared at his hands. He was still there. He couldn't make sense of it.

Luger took advantage of the distraction and upended

Jacob. He landed on top of Jacob and pulled a dagger out of his robe and pressed it to Jacob's throat. Sarah screamed.

"*Non!*" Jacob heard someone shout.

He looked over. It was Napoleon. He held a musket over his head. "*Arrière!*"

"Sir, could we have a chat for a moment?" Phil said in a gentle voice as he stepped up to Napoleon. "Let's talk about your anger. I'm concerned that you are resorting to violence to resolve your inner turmoil."

Napoleon shouldered his musket and aimed it at Luger, who scrambled off of Jacob and dashed over a hill. Jacob quickly ducked away as well. He didn't trust Napoleon's aim.

The Astrals had scattered around. Some were braving the flames and trying to save items from the wreckage and others were staring at the smoldering metal, crying. But Jacob saw determination in their crossed arms and firm jaws. He knew they wouldn't let this setback stop them. They'd build another spaceship, and another after that one if it didn't work.

That's why he was still there, he realized. One setback couldn't stop the Astrals. They would find a way to space no matter what.

But they were all still in danger as long as Luger had the time machine.

Jacob regrouped with Sarah and Mick and they charged after Luger. As they ran over a hill, they saw him standing on a craggy rock, holding his rapier in front of him. He smiled.

"I would be thrilled to see what would happen if you were to come closer."

Suddenly the caveman appeared. "Eedot!" he shouted. He held his club and tapped it on his hands.

"The path to nonviolence is like water flowing over rocks," Phil said as he stood beside the children. "It is the—"

"We know, Phil," Sarah said.

Luger stepped off the rock and crept menacingly toward the children. "You may think you have won, as the Astrals haven't perished. You may believe you can stop me. You cannot. I will do everything within my power to make sure every Astral—"

Jacob saw a blinding flash of prehistoric green. In a flying leap, Nelly lunged for the key in Luger's hand, wrested it from his hand, and sped away with it. Nelly suddenly stopped and stared at the children with the key in his mouth. Then he spit it out and ran away.

Luger started running toward the key, but Napoleon cocked his musket and aimed.

"*Halte!*" Napoleon shouted.

"Oo!" Eedot yelled.

Luger stopped and turned back to face them. He didn't dare make a move toward the key. His shoulders slumped and his face was pale.

Jacob knew they had won.

"Children . . ." an adult said.

Jacob looked over. It was Sarah's parents. They looked shaken, and Jacob knew they had seen everything that had just happened, including the spaceship exploding and Luger threatening them with the sword. Jacob wondered for a second if Sarah's parents would try to grab the time machine and give it back to Luger if their belief in the Strangers was really that strong.

Mick made a dash for the time machine and Sarah stepped over to Jacob and put her arm around his shoulder. "You can't stop me from being Jacob's friend."

"Yeah," Chloe agreed.

Sarah's parents exchanged a glance. "Your mother and I have a lot to think about," Sarah's dad said. "We thought Luger wanted to save Earth from Astrals, not . . . wage a war."

Everyone stood for a moment in silence before Sarah's dad stepped over and gave Sarah and Jacob a hug.

"But we're just glad you're safe."

Chapter 45

Jacob set to work in the past.

He went back to prehistoric times and warped Phil and the caveman to the Astral launch in the 1940s so they would be there to help him defeat Luger. He went back to France with Dexter, who explained to Napoleon the danger they were in, and warped him forward so he'd be there too. He snuck up on Sarah's parents and warped them so they could see precisely how horrible Luger Smythe really was.

He warped to the clearing in the forest on May 16, and found himself face-to-face with Nelly, who twitched a little and stared at Jacob with alert curiosity in his lizard eyes. Nelly blinked. Jacob blinked.

He lunged for Nelly, who tried to bolt away, but

somehow Jacob was able to grab hold of one scaly foot. He warped him back to the 1940s too.

Jacob went back to the morning of May 16 and found Chloe skipping toward school. He stopped her and told her that he was sending her back in time and to tell him that they needed to keep an eye on her. Everything depended on it. She just rolled her eyes and clearly didn't believe him, but he warped her anyway so she would meet them in the past at the right time and they would bring her along on their adventures.

He knew she'd make a mess of things, but if Chloe hadn't been in the Jurassic era, they wouldn't have accidentally warped Nelly into the future, and if Nelly wasn't in the future, Jacob wouldn't have had the idea to use the crazy dinosaur to defeat Luger.

But even as Jacob set things up one by one, there was still something that wasn't quite right. The present was still a mess of tangled jungle. Dexter was still one year older. It wasn't how things were supposed to have unfolded.

In order to set things truly right, he had to fix the original mistake that set everything in motion: Mick's battle against the Strangers.

If Mick hadn't started messing with the past, Jacob wouldn't have gone and seen dinosaurs and accidentally

warped Nelly to the future. Dexter wouldn't have gotten stuck in France and set things off course. Luger wouldn't have gotten his hands on a time machine.

It all started with Mick stranding Jacob's dad in the past. That's what set off the craziness.

If Jacob could stop Mick's plot, everything would go back to normal. Instead of chasing dinosaurs, Jacob would go home and go back to school like a normal kid. The Astrals might never be out of danger from the Strangers, but instead of getting his hands on a time machine and blowing up a spaceship, Luger Smythe would just live out his life in the Tower of London.

Jacob warped back to the clearing down the street from his house the night his dad left home.

He found Mick and his dad arguing in front of his next-door neighbor's house. His dad raised his hands in panic. "Don't do this, Cracken. You don't know what you're messing with. You have to let the past just happen."

Mick shook his head and gave Jacob's dad a cocky grin. "You've gone soft, old man. I'm not going to try and make friends with people who want us all dead. I'm going to beat them once and for all."

"Mick," Jacob's father pleaded. "Don't leave me here. You don't have the experience. You can't try and alter history like this. It will be a disaster."

"It won't be a disaster for Jacob," Mick said.

"Maybe you can go be the dad he wanted this time."

Jacob knew better now. His dad was right. It really wasn't going to work. Despite his good intentions, Mick's attempts to rid themselves of the Strangers was destined to backfire. Even though he'd kept insisting he had a plan, he didn't have much of one beyond enlisting Jacob for help and hoping he could talk and prank his way to success.

And Jacob had to give up on wishing for a different childhood. He had to accept the one he had, as painful as that was. He had to give up the past he wanted for a future he knew would be promising. The pain he felt when his dad left had made him strong. It gave him the strength to do what was right.

Jacob stepped out into the open. "I come from the future," he said ominously, smiling as he remembered from so long ago when he heard Chloe say the same thing in the Jurassic era.

"Jacob . . ." his dad sputtered. Jacob shook his head. It wasn't the time for a reunion. Instead he turned his attention to the space pirate.

"Mick," Jacob said. "You can't do this. It's not going to work."

Jacob patted Mick on the shoulder and enjoyed his startled expression.

"The past is the past."

Chapter 46

Jacob, Sarah, Chloe, Dexter, Catalina, and Mick sat on a blanket on a hill overlooking a magnificent, ramshackle steel spaceship. The past had been set right. History had unfolded as it should. The Astrals weren't in danger from Luger Smythe, and the neighborhood where the houses looked the same had the gray sidewalks and messy lawns that Jacob had known all his life.

Jacob's dad had let them borrow the time machine to watch this one amazing event as long as they didn't talk to anybody and change anything that would happen.

"So . . . let me get this straight," Dexter said. "We didn't go back to see dinosaurs. And I never met Bonnie. And I'm a normal age now."

"That's right," Jacob said.

"Then how come I can remember it?" Dexter asked.

"Because you did do it once," Jacob said. "You just didn't do it in the history we're living in now."

Dexter rubbed his eyes. "My head hurts."

They all stood up and huddled closely together to listen when Father Albert gave his speech about the future of the Astrals, and watched the Astrals climb excitedly into the spaceship. The Astrals weren't safe from all the people who wished them harm in the universe, but the children had to trust that good would ultimately prevail in the end.

They counted down as smoke emerged from the rockets, and stood up and cheered when the spaceship shot like a bullet into the sky. The Astrals left Earth safely to start their magical civilization. They weren't out of danger from the Strangers, but Jacob was hopeful the reasonable people on both sides would continue to find a way to make sure they all lived in peace.

The kids sat there for a moment in the darkness, watching the embers in the grass burn down. Jacob lay back onto the hill, shoulder-to-shoulder with Sarah, and stared up at the stars, hoping he'd soon have a chance to return to them.

"New idea," Mick said. "What if we warped back and put maggots in Luger Smythe's bed?"

Chloe groaned. "Mr. Wonderbar said we could warp back to watch the Astral launch, and *that's it*. Final. End of story."

Mick was quiet for a moment. "But I'm president of the universe!"

"Too bad," Sarah said. She leaned over and winked at Chloe.

"Here's what I still don't get," Jacob said. "I understand there were actually three time machines, but how did you warp us *and* Praiseworthy fifty years into the future?"

He leaned on one elbow and watched Mick try to suppress a smile. It was the trademark Mick Cracken smile that said: "I'm the world's biggest genius." Mick was unable to stop himself from smiling and he started laughing.

"Come on, Wonderbar, you don't know?"

Jacob leaned back onto the blanket. "No," he said through gritted teeth. "Why don't you tell me what an incredible thinker you are?"

"How do you start a spaceship?" Mick asked.

Jacob thought back to the night a year ago in the forest when he traded the man in silver a corndog for a spaceship. "With . . . a key," Jacob said.

Mick cackled. "Let's just say I used one of the *special* keys for your return trip. And I programmed Praiseworthy to say the magic words."

"I hate you," Sarah said.

"No, you don't," Mick said.

Jacob stood up and brushed the grass off of his pants. "We should go," he said, though a part of him felt hollow when he said it. He and Sarah and Chloe and Dexter had to go back to Earth and start their normal lives again, with schoolwork and extra-curriculars and chores and teachers, while Mick and Catalina were off to run the universe as president and vice president. It wouldn't be the same. Jacob was relieved that they wouldn't be running around through time and trying to save a civilization, but he would miss being with all of his true friends.

Everyone stood up and they joined together in a circle, their arms around one another.

Jacob thrust his hand into the middle of the circle. "Space friends forever?"

Mick, Sarah, Catalina, Chloe, and Dexter placed their hands on top of Jacob's. "Space friends forever!" they shouted.

When they warped back into the clearing in the forest down the street, the spaceship Praiseworthy and Jacob's dad were waiting for them. Jacob dutifully handed over the time machine to his father. Chloe and Catalina had tears in their eyes, and when Jacob's dad saw them, he cleared his throat and said, "I'll give you guys a moment."

Jacob hugged Catalina, who grasped him so tight, he could barely breathe. He whispered, "Hope to see you soon."

Catalina broke the hug and nodded.

Then he clasped Mick's hand in a handshake but broke it and he gave him a hug too, clapping him on the back hard enough that he hoped it hurt a little.

"My man," Jacob said.

Mick laughed and looked Jacob in the eye. He tipped up his chin. "It's been fun."

Sarah hugged Mick and Catalina hugged Dexter and it felt like it was too soon, but then Mick and

Catalina climbed into the spaceship Praiseworthy, waving their last good-byes.

Then, with a slight stirring and the quietest of whirs, the spaceship Praiseworthy launched into the sky and disappeared into the night.

Chapter 47

When Jacob returned to the sidewalk on the street where all the houses looked the same, his dad was nowhere to be found.

Jacob felt a flush of anger when he remembered the peculiar expression on his dad's face when he made his exit after seeing Sarah and Catalina crying. He had looked guilty. His dad never was good at good-byes, and once again he had slipped away just as suddenly as he had appeared. It almost felt like a dream. Jacob had only had a short period where he had seen his dad and talked to him and now he was gone.

But Jacob had gotten by without his dad for two years, and he was a stronger person. There was nothing he could do about it, but he knew he would get through it.

The children had warped back to the same night, way back, when they had blasted off so Jacob could run for president of the universe. Their parents would never know they had ever left, but so much time had passed and Jacob felt like a vastly different person. He wondered if his mom would even recognize him.

"So I guess my mom is going to be in the hospital soon," Dexter said.

"Wait, what?" Jacob said.

"Oh!" Sarah said. "Jake, while you and Mick were who knows where in time we found out Dexter's mom is going to be sick. But don't worry, she's going to be okay."

"Thank goodness," Jacob said. "But hey, Dexter?"

Dexter stopped. "Yeah?"

"We'll be there. You won't have to go through that alone."

Dexter nodded and smiled. "I know. Thanks, guys."

"Me too, Dexy," Chloe said.

Dexter closed his eyes. "I just . . ." He turned away and walked toward home.

When it was time for Sarah and Chloe to turn home, Chloe punched Jacob on the shoulder. "Smell ya later!"

"Bye, Chloe," Jacob said through gritted teeth.

Then Sarah enveloped him in a hug. "You're the

best," she whispered. "You know that, right? The very best."

"I'm so lucky," Jacob said. "Really lucky."

Sarah grinned. "I know you are."

Sarah started walking home and she elbowed Chloe and they shared a laugh. Jacob wasn't sure he would ever get used to the sight of Sarah and Chloe getting along.

Jacob walked home, and a part of him was nervous that one last trick had been played. The last time he had come home after a long adventure, his mom was fifty years older. He wondered if he would arrive to find her as a teenager or maybe Jacob would meet his grandparents or who knows what.

He reached their doorstep and stared at the old faded wreath on the door. He pulled it off and hid it behind a bush. It was time to get rid of that thing.

He took a deep breath and walked in the door. "Mom?" he called out.

"Hi, darling," she said.

Jacob rounded the corner and saw his mom sitting at the dining room table. With his dad.

"Your father is in town and decided to join us for dinner," she said. "Isn't that . . . nice?"

"If it's okay with you," his dad said.

Jacob sat down wordlessly. His mom handed him a

bowl full of a mysterious green sludge and he scooped some of it onto his plate and stared at it. He couldn't believe he was sitting at the same table as his mother and his father. They seemed somewhat tense around each other, but Jacob could tell they were making an effort on his behalf.

"Isn't this a surprise?" his mom said. "Hopefully your father will visit his *son* a bit more often." She glared at him and Jacob's dad stared at his food as if he were trying to make a positive scientific identification of a strange and unknown life form.

Then Jacob's dad looked at Jacob and nodded. "I'm going to try."

"Okay . . ." Jacob said.

He stared at his plate for a moment without eating anything.

"Can I ask you guys a question?"

"Shoot," his dad said.

"How many adults know about space?" Jacob said.

Jacob's mom and dad exchanged a smile as if they had been expecting that question. Jacob surmised that his dad had caught his mom up on what had happened. "Lots of people know," his dad said. "But lots more refuse to believe what's right in front of them."

Jacob poked at his food and thought about all those

UFO videos on YouTube. He certainly never believed there was anything to those crazy rumors until he saw the spaceship in the forest down the street. Now he knew there was an incredible civilization living among the stars.

"Why were the Daisys mixed up with the Strangers?"

Jacob's mom froze. "You know about that too?"

"Yeah," Jacob said. "What happened? How did they even find out you're an Astral?"

"Well . . . there was an incident," Jacob's mom said. "One of your father's spaceships accidentally landed in the Daisys' backyard. It caused quite a bit of tension between us when they found out the truth about your father. The Goldsteins spoke up on your father's behalf and there was a big falling out."

"But why were the Daisys involved with the Strangers?" Jacob asked.

Jacob's dad shook his head. "There's no easy answer. We all started out as friends, but when Sarah and Chloe were young, the Daisys started worrying that they had an Astral living down the street. They started believing those crazy stories the Strangers tell about what Astrals do to Earthers. They always thought I was up to no good. I think they felt safer thinking they had other Strangers to protect them. Sometimes people let their fear get the best of them. Even good people can get carried away."

Jacob thought about it for a moment and swallowed a bite of his mom's dinner. It didn't taste very good, but he didn't want to go hungry.

Later that night, Jacob stared out his window at the starry sky and wondered when he would again be able to fly between planets and travel through time and have adventures with Mick and Catalina. It would be difficult to go back to school and sit through math lectures and do homework, knowing that just days ago he had been trying to save the Astral civilization and seeing things his classmates could only dream of. Dinosaurs and cavemen and Napoleon's coronation and a beautiful rocket ship blasting off into space with the dreams of the Astral civilization on board.

He wasn't sure if he could believe that his dad really was going to be a part of his life, and he felt some part of himself steeling himself against disappointment. He had spent so long experiencing the worst with his dad, he wasn't able to believe that things may be taking a turn for the better. He might be able to hope again.

Jacob heard a knock at his door. "Jacob?" His dad peeked through. "Oh, hey. Listen, since it's Saturday tomorrow, I was thinking pancakes for breakfast, how does that sound?"

Jacob smiled and nodded. He had been craving his dad's pancakes for a long, long time.

"Great." His dad smiled. "I'll see you tomorrow.

Jacob had traveled billions of miles and through thousands of years looking for his dad. And for the first time in all those years he felt like he had really found him.

It wasn't perfect. But it was a start.

ACKNOWLEDGMENTS

Jacob Wonderbar and the Interstellar Time Warp wouldn't have made it into the present without my incredible team:

TELEPORTATION: I'm incredibly lucky to have my wonderful agent, Catherine Drayton, and the incomparable Kate Harrison, my editor, who made these books real.

CATALYSTS: Thanks to Heather Alexander, Patricia Burke, Lyndsey Blessing, Alexis Hurley, Nathaniel Jacks, and Charlie Olson for their hard work on all three Jacob Wonderbar novels.

SOURCE: Big thanks to Jacob and Phil Jaber of Philz Coffee of San Francisco for their generous encouragement and for creating Jacob's Wonderbar brew.

SCHEMATICS: Thanks to Christopher S. Jennings (illustrations), Jasmin Rubero (interior), and Greg Stadnyk (cover) for bringing the books to life.

SUPPORT: These books would not be possible without my amazing friends. Thanks to Egya Appiah, Justin Berkman, Lisa Brackmann, Holly Burns, Madissen De Turris, Christian DiCarlo, Emily Dreyfuss, Dan Goldstein, Jennifer Hubbard, Mark Kaufman, Matt Lasner, Sommer Leigh, Tahereh Mafi, Maggie Mason, Sarah McCarry, Bryan Russell, Karen Schennum, Sean Slinsky, Sharon Vaknin, Meg Wilkinson, my blog readers and forumites, and everyone at CNET.

NUCLEUS: Thanks to Mom, Dad, Darcie, Mike, Scott, and Beth for being the best family in the universe.